D1065189

# Cadbury's Coffin

## By Glendon & Kathryn Swarthout

THE GHOST AND THE MAGIC SABER

WHICHAWAY

THE BUTTON BOAT

TV THOMPSON

WHALES TO SEE THE

## By Glendon Swarthout

WILLOW RUN

THEY CAME TO CORDURA

WHERE THE BOYS ARE

WELCOME TO THEBES

THE CADILLAC COWBOYS

THE EAGLE AND THE IRON CROSS

LOVELAND

BLESS THE BEASTS AND CHILDREN

THE TIN LIZZIE TROOP

LUCK AND PLUCK

THE SHOOTIST

THE MELODEON

SKELETONS

## By Kathryn Swarthout

LIFESAVORS

# Cadbury's Coffin

*Glendon and Kathryn Swarthout*

DOUBLEDAY & COMPANY, INC.
Garden City, New York
1982

Library of Congress Cataloging in Publication Data

Swarthout, Glendon Fred.
Cadbury's coffin.

Summary: Greedy relatives and scheming servants come
to battle over the will of a cantankerous old tycoon, as
he lies on his deathbed and later in his tomb, where he
may have been placed prematurely.
[1. Mystery and detective stories.   2. Inheritance
and succession—Fiction]   I. Swarthout, Kathryn.
II. Title.
PZ7.S9727Cad      [Fic]
AACR2
ISBN: 0-385-17578-7
Library of Congress Catalog Card Number 81–43590

Text copyright © 1982 by Glendon & Kathryn Swarthout
Illustrations copyright © 1982 by Doubleday & Company, Inc.

ALL RIGHTS RESERVED
PRINTED IN THE UNITED STATES OF AMERICA
FIRST EDITION

# Contents

# List of Illustrations

He who shall teach the child to doubt
The rotting grave shall ne'er get out.

*William Blake*

# Cadbury's Coffin

*In his nightcap and shirt, his legs askew, he seemed
shrunken, no bigger than a doll.*

# 1

# An Oak Tree Topples

he night makes infants of us all. It is in the late and faltering hours before the cock crows, before dawn blesses us to rest again, that we are most afraid, and never more alone. We do not sleep, nor dare not dream. Seconds shuffle. Minutes plod. The tick of a clock, the warmth of a pillow, the nearness and dearness of fathers, mothers, sisters, brothers—these console us not. The darkness diminishes us. Sealed in sheets as in a grave, we seem small and weak and helpless. We hear things. We see things. We wait, for what we must not imagine. We hang, somewhere between that which has been and that which will be, by a slender thread.

*For it is then we know that our lives are but a brief recess after night, before another endless night. It is then we know, young and old alike, that one day we will die.*

Minnie Pumpley lay in her bed, listening. It was three or four o'clock in the morning, and time for him to be up and about, to unsettle everyone. He slept by fits and starts, as the elderly were wont to do, and more by day than by night; and he had begun of late to rise in the wee hours and ramble. This was dangerous. In the dark he could tumble headlong down the circling staircase. He could kill himself. And so, over his objections, they had moved him downstairs, turning his library, off which there was a bathroom, into a bed-sitting room. Now he might prowl as he pleased, disturbing though it was to others. Little did he care. But his "rambling," as Minnie called it, was only one of his new and unpleasant practices. Mentally he was quick and shrewd as ever—his clerks came regularly to the mansion to report to him on production and profits at the works, and woe to them if their accounting were incomplete. Temperamentally, however, he had become cantankerous, even vile. He crabbed about his new false teeth, of porcelain mounted on a vulcanized rubber base, and often refused to wear them—then crabbed at her for preparing meats he could not chew. He pinched her backside on the opportunity, then cackled with glee. He was frequently mean to his pets. He objected to bathing beyond once a week and last week hurled a bar of soap from the tub through a windowpane. In the past he had taken care to use the cuspidors, but more than seldom recently she had caught him lifting a corner of an oriental rug, spitting tobacco juice on the parquet floor beneath, and dropping the corner to conceal it. This, in her opinion, was downright nasty.

Minnie Pumpley sighed, turned in her bed, and listened to the squeak of springs, to the mumbles in the room next hers, to the brush of tree branches against brick wall. Then she heard him. Unless one were accustomed to the sounds downstairs, they would give a body the shakes. He was up, having groaned himself out of bed in nightcap and shirt and bare feet. Thump-thump-thump went his canes, one in each hand, as he doddered into the parlor. Now he would ramble from room to room talking to himself, peering out windows, accepting and rejecting the attentions of his pets, thumping, thinking. What did old men think about in the night? Death? Money? Their heirs? What the Hereafter held in store for them? Would they not tot up the deeds of their days, and pray the good outweighed the bad?

Eli Stamp heard him, too. Eli was afflicted with lumbago, rheumatic pain in the lower back. Each time he changed position in his bed, the pain roused him; his sleep was consequently fitful, alternating between dream and drowse, past and present. It was he whose mumbles had been audible to Mrs. Pumpley in the room next his.

He listened. His hearing was not what it once had been, but the thump-thump-thump of canes downstairs recalled to him the staccato of soldiers' makeshift

crutches on a wooden trestle bridge. He puzzled why it
had not yet snowed. This was late November, almost
December. They should have had a foot of snow by
now; the boy should have been tied to a shovel like a
pup. He dozed again. In his dream he heard the boom
of cannon, the whine of grapeshot through thickets in
the Wilderness, and the thump of wounded comrades'
crutches as they limped from battle across a bridge in
Virginia.

Verbena Huttle heard him, too. At fifteen she was a
sound sleeper, but even the blissful oblivion of youth
was not impervious to the high-pitched yowl which
started from the dining room, rang through the
kitchen, and quavered, finally, up the narrow crooked
stairway to her small bedroom on the other side of Eli
Stamp's. He had struck a cat with a cane. How many
cats enjoyed his hospitality no one could tell; she had
counted nineteen once, sixteen once, twenty-one another
time. He welcomed strays. He insisted they be fed and
given the run of the place, be let out by day and
gathered again into his fold at dusk. They were children to him. And they showed their gratitude by prom-
enading with him at night, purring in chorus as he
talked to himself, twining and rubbing his bare, spindly
legs. When this demonstration resulted in his loss of
balance, and he feared falling, he would brace himself
with one cane and flail at them with the other. Usually
he missed the mark, and would punish them with
oaths; but occasionally his aim was true, and one of
them, it did not matter which, would bear the full

brunt of his displeasure. Childless he might have been in real life, but if he spoiled these creature substitutes, who mewled and swilled milk by the gallon and clawed upholstery to shreds, that was his right. Certainly no one could claim he spared the rod.

Verbena Huttle disliked the nights she slept in the mansion. Her bed was comfortable enough, and she had it to herself rather than sharing it, as she did at home, with two bratty sisters. But she dreaded the middle of these mansion nights—the fingering of his canes along the floors, the protests of his pets, the whimper of wind in the gables and about the chimneys as it seemed to beg for entrance. She shivered. She hugged herself.

It was the outcry of another cat which waked young Joshua Overland. His bed was a straw tick in a cubbyhole at the head of the stairway from the kitchen. He simply could not accustom himself to these night sounds. He tossed and twisted. He wanted to yowl himself, to demand that the man downstairs get the dickens back to bed where all sensible folk belonged at this hour.

And so, listening, waiting, they lay in their beds in the servants' quarters at three or four o'clock in the morning—Minnie Pumpley, Eli Stamp, Verbena Huttle, and Joshua Overland.

Suddenly the wind died.

Suddenly silence reigned.

The four tensed. Small and weak and vulnerable now, each one alone, they held breath.

Did they not, in the dark of night, grow cold with

apprehension? Were they not, in the dark of night, re-
duced to infants all?

The crash, when it came, was thunderous. It was
mingled with the shatter of glass and the clash of
chimes. It seemed to shake the entire house.

Joshua Overland was first out of bed. The place in
which he slept was a cramped, musty space used for-
merly to store trunks and valises, open at the hall end
and lacking a window, and so low was the ceiling that
in order to exit he must crawl or crack his head. He
crawled out now and hesitated in his union suit at the
head of the stairs, unwilling to descend for fear of what
he might find. Down the hall he heard old Eli's grum-
ble, the plaint of Verbena's girlish voice, questioning,
then Mrs. Pumpley's urgent hiss:
"Go down and see, you ninny!"
It sent him down, step by step, into the kitchen to
the electric light switch; then, blinking, into the dining
room; then to the door of the great parlor where,
reaching round the jamb, his fingers felt for another
switch, found it, and turned it.
He gasped.
Lycurgus Cadbury lay on the floor.
In his nightcap and shirt, his legs askew, he seemed
shrunken, no bigger than a doll.
His eyes were closed. From one corner of his open,
toothless mouth a ribbon of spittle glazed in the light.
His canes had dropped beside him.
Near him, pulled down by him evidently in an at-

tempt to break his fall, lay the grandfather clock. It had been the clock's weight, not the shatter of its glass face and front or the clash of its Whittington chimes, which had seemed to shake the house.

About the parlor, on rugs and sofas and chairs, their yellow eyes attentive, their mewling stilled as though by tragedy, sat a wake of cats.

Lycurgus Cadbury had fallen in his eighty-fourth year. It had been his design, his heart's desire, indeed his obsession, to live at least a while into the new century, the twentieth. He had come up short by a scant thirty-two days. This was the early morning of November 29, in the year 18 and 99.

"Eeeeeeeee!"

Mrs. Pumpley's scream so startled young Josh that he jumped and came down on the tail of a cat. The animal emitted a rasp of resentment which, added to Verbena's moan and old Eli's groan, made the room a babble. The others had crept downstairs and entered the parlor after Josh, had seen now what he had seen, and milled about in horror and confusion.

"Poor Mr. Cadbury!" moaned Verbena, rolling her eyes.

"Ohhh! Ohhh!" groaned Eli Stamp, shaking his head.

"I knew it! I knew it!" cried Mrs. Pumpley, hands at her cheeks. "Mercy of God!"

Widow she might be, but married she had been to the household for thirty years, in sickness and in health, for better or for worse. And in another minute she had them bustling—Verbena to the telephone in the entry to ring up Dr. Hopkins and say that Mr. Cadbury was dead and he must come immediately, Josh and Eli to stand the clock upright, then bring broom and dustpan. This they did, only to discover Verbena did not know how to use the telephone, to crank and contact the operator, so Mrs. Pumpley had to make the call in her stead while Eli swept up shards of glass from the rug and Josh collected the cats one by one and saw them out a side door.

Her parlor put to rights, the pious housekeeper then took them into the dining room, away from the body, ordered them to kneel with her—a feat of contortion for Eli—and recite the Lord's Prayer. This they did as well, after which she asked that each remain in place, head bowed, eyes closed, and devote some time to meditation on the kindness and generosity of the man who had now "gone to his reward," the soul which had already, she was sure, "taken its place amongst the Heavenly Host." How long they so devoted no one knew, but it seemed an age. Verbena sniffled. Mrs. Pumpley sighed. Josh stifled yawns. Eli trembled in every antique limb. And when the doorbell rang, causing even the old soldier to shoot to his feet like a rocket, it was a relief as much as an amen.

Dr. Silas Hopkins was admitted to the parlor. One of only two physicians in Gilead, and of the two by far the more learned in science, he had long cared for Mr. Cadbury. He was fiftyish, a bachelor and a dandy, wiry and vigorous, with penetrating eyes and a waxed mustache, the ends of which he tweaked when immersed in thought. He greeted the four with a nod, removed a hat of black seal fur and a velvet-collared Chesterfield coat, opened his black bag, rubbed his hands, and got down to grim business.

He placed a hand on the corpse's chest.

He looked at the servants.

"He has not expired," he said.

They gaped at him.

"He is not dead."

They gaped at each other. Minnie Pumpley backed into a chair and sat down heavily.

The doctor then peered into his patient's eyes, taking care to note the angle of the retinas. Extracting a rubber mallet from his bag, he tapped elbows and legs for reflex. He twisted the left leg, then the right, to ascertain a fracture of either hip in the fall. At length he rose, tweaked an end of his mustache for a moment, and made his diagnosis.

"Mr. Cadbury has incurred a cerebral hemorrhage," he said. "In common parlance, a stroke. A thrombosis, or blood clot, in one hemisphere of the brain which blocks the circulation of the blood. I cannot tell as yet if there will be paralysis, loss of speech, so on."

He paused, and addressed them soberly. "In any event, his condition is critical. He is elderly, he is frail, and my best guess is that he has precious little time. I would advise you to summon his nieces at once." He looked at young Overland. "Josh, isn't it?"

"Yes, sir."

"You appear able-bodied. Let's get him into bed."

With maid and housekeeper carrying canes and hov-

ering, Josh and the doctor lifted the comatose Lycurgus Cadbury, who was light as a feather, carried
him into his room off the parlor, and deposited him
gingerly in bed.

"Should I sit with him?" whispered Mrs. Pumpley.

"It won't be necessary," was the response. "I'll look
in on him in the morning, when he's conscious and
when I can better tell what damage has been done."

They returned to the parlor. Briskly the doctor
donned his coat and hat. "I repeat," he said. "I would
urge Miss Hetta Mae and Mrs. Morgan to make haste
—and to come prepared to stay till the end."

"You mean he—" began Mrs. Pumpley.

"I do."

To their surprise, young Josh spoke up, having done
some arithmetic. "Pardon me, sir, but could he—could
he live thirty-two days?"

Black bag in hand, Silas Hopkins turned at the door.
"Into the next century? Ah, yes, I recall his ambition. I
think not, Josh. No, having achieved everything else he
wanted in life, for once Mr. Cadbury has failed." He
frowned. "I'm sorry. But I doubt he will be with us
thirty-two hours."

A clock ticked. It was after four o'clock in the morning. Alone again, the four of them were drinking cocoa,
a treat they would never have dared, night or day, had
their employer been in good health. They sat in the chilly
kitchen, their faces pale, their eyes hollowed from want
of sleep.

Eli sucked greedily at his cocoa. He was hairless.

Drawn taut over his old skull, the skin gleamed. His nightshirt looked to have been slept in for months without a change, and round his skinny neck he had safety-pinned a woolen sock tinctured with drops of camphor to ward off the ague, a fever to which he claimed soldiers were frequently subject. No one knew Eli's age, and he himself had forgotten, but he was a veteran of the Civil War, had been the oldest man in Gilead to volunteer, and had seen two years of service with the Second New York Zouaves, a regiment of infantry whose ranks were decimated in Virginia. There, in the Wilderness, where men were slaughtered by the thousands on both sides, Union and Confederate, he had taken a minié ball through the shoulder, and was invalided home. The shoulder healed and stiffened. Because he could no longer earn his living at what was then the Cadbury Wagon Works, his patriotism was rewarded by the offer of a position with his former employer in his own household, and here he had toiled as coachman-handyman-gardener as long as Minnie Pumpley, and for the same pay—ten dollars a month and found.

Of the camphor, only Mrs. Pumpley was unaware. Her face, Josh had thought on first meeting it, was like that of a basset hound, loyal and friendly; and in return for loyalty and friendship she would wag her tail forever. But at this hour she slumped, her plump cheeks sagged, the cup between her elbows was ignored. As her bosom burdened the table, the masses of her coarse gray hair, compacted into a bun during the day, burdened her broad shoulders. She wore carpet slippers and a flannel bathrobe with a rose print, the flowers as faded and drear as her expression. She was a woman worn to the bone.

Mr. Cadbury had of late tested her loyalty to the utmost. She had suffered him. He was old, and changes of habit and character all too often accompanied advanced age. She was sixty-three herself, and sadly conscious of swelling about her knees and ankles, the first signs of dropsy. These, too, she must endure, as she had Mr. Cadbury's transformation, for she had been his cook-housekeeper nigh on thirty years—ten before he was widowed and twenty since, first in the old house, torn down, and later in this mansion, built five years ago to replace it. They had been, on the whole, good years. She had been in sole charge of a banquet in 1882 for Chester A. Arthur, President of the United States, who was an overnight guest in the old house, and he had complimented her on the roast boar. Later that hot July night there was an electrical storm, and at about this time a bolt of lightning struck a huge oak tree on the lawn, and rived it so that half the trunk and limbs toppled against brick wall and alarmed everyone out of bed, including President Arthur. It shook the entire house.

Verbena Huttle sat at the table sipping. She was a slight girl, and the wash-worn challis nightgown lent her by Mrs. Pumpley was so capacious that she tied it about her waist with a string. Her blond hair was done up in rag curlers. Her dimples were deep, even when her heart-shaped face was in repose. She was prone to roll her violet eyes, and over the rim of her cup she rolled them now, sometimes at Josh, sometimes at the others, but oftener at Josh.

She was the eldest of ten children. When she turned fifteen, and it was apparent her father was unequal to the task of providing for his brood, she was presented with the choice of applying at the Cadbury Cutter Works, which was Gilead's only industry, or of going into domestic service. The one was a dead end, the other an unknown; but at least, if she could find the right place, it might uplift her someday to a height she could never aspire to in a manufactory. She might even become a family favorite. She might even marry a rich man.

Hence it was innocence which took her forthwith to "the mansion," as it was invariably referred to; it was innocence which propelled her by the wide lawns and up the circle drive under magnificent oaks and elms, past the cutter, or sleigh, parked prominently in front, a life-sized, single-seater replica made of iron and drawn by an iron steed. This was the largest home for miles around. House and stable and grassy, shaded sweeps occupied a whole town block. A fortress of red brick boasting six rooms down and seven up, it was roofed with terne metal, the edges protected by metal shingles individually stamped in the form of oak leaves. There were high chimneys and gables and dormer windows and in one corner, crowned by a gilded weather vane, a glassed-in cupola, or "sea watch," from which one could espy, on a clear day, Troy to the southeast and Albany to the southwest. There were porches on two sides, long and painted green and trimmed with intri-

cate wooden scrollwork. Innocence sent Miss Huttle up
the asphalt drive, up the wide steps, over the broad ve-
randa to the front door rather than the rear, manda-
tory entrance for servants and deliveries. Innocence let
her ring the bell. Fortune, in the person of a Mrs.
Pumpley, swelling at the knees and ankles, and dis-
traught that morning with responsibility, let her in.

She was happy. She was paid five dollars a month
and allowed lunch, for she was day help. Only now and
again, when she must work late, as she had today, was
she given supper and a bed. She was housemaid and
scullery maid. She dusted, swept, scrubbed, mopped,
waxed, polished, and beat; she cut, whipped, sliced,
stirred, scoured, washed, and dried—all these twelve
hours at a stretch, seven days of the week. But no matter how toilsome the time, how menial the drudgery,
the mansion to her was a castle, and she could pretend,
even while cleaning up after cats, that she was a prin-
cess. She admired the beveled glass windows, the brass
hardware copper-flashed throughout, the transom of
stained glass over every interior door; and she was
amazed by such modernities as electric lights and a
telephone and the "window doors" which would, on the
pressure of a hand, rise into the walls and provide in
summer a marvelous means of ventilation. She loved
the molded metal ceilings, the height and spaciousness
of the rooms, the luxury of the furnishings. And she
liked Mrs. Pumpley and old Eli and Josh—especially
Josh. Secretly she wished he were two or three years
older. How handsome he would be then! How eligible!

He sat on a stool in his union suit, one bare foot atop

the other, his brown hair a rat's nest. His open countenance was freckled, his ears were large, his chin was cleft, and his hands and wrists were broad and strong for one of fourteen—tribute to the tons of coal, snow, wood, and horse manure he had moved from one place to another.

At this moment Josh was sorry he could not feel for his employer the sympathy he might have for a father, but filial devotion was a subject in which life had little schooled him. He had never known a father, or a mother for that matter. Entrusted to the doorstep of an orphanage in Albany when only days old, he had eked out an existence there, instructed in the rudiments of reading, writing, and ciphering, until he was twelve. Destiny then, or chance, took him by the nape of the neck. He was plucked away to act as helper to an old man named Eli Stamp, who served in a great house in Gilead. He was given a straw tick, a cubbyhole, clothing, board, five dollars a month—and given to understand that should he fail or be slack in the performance of his duties before he was sixteen, at which age he might legally be released as a charge of the state of New York, back to the orphanage he would go.

Joshua Overland was a boy of sterling qualities, amiable disposition, and sturdy physique. And it was well that he was sturdy, for as Eli became ever more infirm, the ancient found ever more for his assistant to do. Josh was what was termed a "chore boy." From breakfast to bed, in fair weather and foul, he whirled like a dervish. He cared for horses and harness, cleaned stables, mowed lawns, raked and burned leaves, shoveled

snow, toted wood for six fireplaces and the kitchen
stove, coaled the monster furnace in the basement,
banked it at night, grated and hauled the ashes in the
morning, aided Mrs. Pumpley when ordered, and
sprang to Verbena's side at the slightest pallor in her
cheek, at the merest dither of her lashes. How like an
angel she was, an angel he had once seen in a picture
book depicting the differences between Heaven and
Hell. How he wished he were two or three years older!

Eli smacked his lips. "Aye, Master be took this
time." He spoke to himself. "Stroke's sure as shootin'.
That I know."

"I knew it, too, soon's I heard that crash," agreed
Mrs. Pumpley. "Like that old oak tree, way back
then."

"You called them women?" he asked.

"The both of 'em. Miss Hetta Mae first, she being
the closest."

Hetta Mae Cadbury lived in Gloversville, only
twenty miles from Gilead.

"Did she faint?" inquired Verbena.

"I thought she did. Not a peep out of 'er for a long
spell. Then she come on the line again and said she'll
hire a trap and be here by ten. Oh, I'll bet she will,
cryin' over him like spilt milk." Mrs. Pumpley remembered her cocoa, warmed herself with it, then warmed
to the telling. "Then I called Mrs. Morgan. I never
called to New York City before; he always did it. You
can hear the wires hum. I told her, and nary a peep
from her neither for a bit. I could hear her thinkin',
though. She'll come up on the train, she said, her and

Montfort. Be here by noon." She sighed. "What we'll have to put up with these next few days—great sakes." She reflected. "Oh, they'll come on the run, all right. Money. Which of 'em'll get the most when he's gone."

Josh piped up again. "Mrs. Pumpley, how rich is Mr. Cadbury?"

She stared at him.

"It ain't snowed yet," declared Eli. "Why don't it snow?"

"How rich is he?" Josh repeated.

Verbena stared at him.

"Never you mind," responded Mrs. Pumpley. "None of our business. Everybody says he's a millionaire—how muchever that is."

Verbena took courage. "Might he—might he leave us something?"

Mrs. Pumpley stared at her.

"Might he?" the girl repeated.

Josh stared at her.

"No," said the housekeeper. "He might, bein' a good and righteous man—but there won't be naught to leave after them two get their hands in his pockets."

She had said too much, and knew it, and pressed her lips into a line, and the room grew still, and chiller still. A clock ticked. The cocoa cups were empty. The last words of Dr. Hopkins echoed in the minds of the four: "I doubt he will be with us thirty-two hours." And it was now that the realization of what this night might mean to them assailed their hearts as the smell of camphor did their nostrils. Each of them realized, as never before, how utterly dependent he was, she was, upon Lycurgus Cadbury. As long as the man drew breath, as long as his feeble mechanisms functioned, they were safe. They had a roof over their heads, and beds to sleep in, and their bellies might anticipate the next meal. But the hour, the minute, the second he ceased to exist, they were lost, cast out into a cruel world penniless, friendless, hopeless—fate's abandoned toys.

A clock ticked. Their cups were empty. Suddenly Minnie Pumpley put her head down on the table, buried her face in her arms, and loosed a lament for all:

"Oh, whatever's to become of us!"

They went to bed. Housekeeper, aged retainer, maid, and chore boy climbed the narrow stairs in that order. At the top, while the others proceeded, Josh touched Verbena on the shoulder. She turned to him. He stood on the step below her, so that small as she was their faces were on a level in the darkness.

"Don't you fret, Verbena," he whispered. "No matter what, I'll take care of you."

"Oh, Josh, thank you," she whispered, and kissed him, and was gone.

*"Now I trip the lever and—presto!"*

# 2
# *Lycurgus Cadbury's Coffin*

n the beginning there had been two brothers, Lycurgus, ten years the senior, and Josephus. Josephus had burned his candle at both ends, marrying early and dying early, of drink and dissipation, but in the interim he sired two daughters, Hetta Mae and Lillian; and although the older brother despised the younger for his vices and his lack of backbone, it was his decision to help the new widow and her little girls. Once come to by Lycurgus, a decision was carried out to the last jot and tittle. He saw to the widow's living until her demise. He provided her daughters with funds sufficient to feed, clothe, house, and educate them, and continued to do so to this day, after both had entered middle life. He considered it

duty rather than charity. He did not love his nieces, and in truth either would have been difficult to love. They were as opposite, and disagreed as violently, as cats and dogs. One would not have known that they were sisters.

Hetta Mae had caused him the lesser expense. She was an old maid, she kept a canary, she lived in a rented house in Gloversville, she did needlepoint, she drank cambric tea, she had horrid dreams about men, she attended church faithfully, she was fifty-two. On the first day of each month she received a check, by way of her uncle's attorney, Brainerd Peckham, in the amount of one hundred dollars, and complained constantly that it was barely enough to keep body and soul together—when the fact was that she lived on it with something to spare. Mr. Cadbury did not increase it.

Lillian, on the other hand, was a chip off her father's block. She lived in an apartment in New York City, she went to the opera, she dressed in the latest fashions, she kept a poodle, she had lovely dreams about some-day living as lavishly as Mrs. Stuyvesant Fish and Mrs. Cornelius Vanderbilt, she adored bonbons, she was forty-seven. Her monthly stipend was three hundred dollars, and she complained constantly to her uncle that on such a sum she could scarcely make ends meet, much less maintain the standard of living to which her husband had accustomed her. Mr. Cadbury did not increase it. But if Lillian was extravagant, she had at least enriched the family with a scandal. She had married Harrison Morgan, a gay blade who speculated in Wall Street. They were man and wife ten years, during

which time he gave her a son, whom she named Montfort, and after which time, to the shock of all concerned, he gave her the slip. Harry Morgan disap-
peared. Some said he had gone to the South Seas with
his strumpet secretary. Others believed he had met a
desperate end, in the sewers of Paris perhaps. In any
event, neither hide nor hair of him had been seen since,
so that Lillian Morgan had lived now for twelve years
in limbo, a wife yet not a wife, widowed yet not a
widow. It had not by any means been the ruination of
her. In fact, she had put on weight.

These three, then, two nieces and the son of one,
were the millionaire's closest relatives, his most direct
descendants, and hence most likely, and logically, his
heirs. As has been said, he did not love them. He made
fun of Hetta Mae behind her back. He complained
constantly that Lillian would spend him out of house
and home. Montfort he judged a piss-ant.

Blood, however, is thicker than water, and Lycurgus
Cadbury was a man to whom blood, family, hard work,
and the Grand Old Party were sacred. And it had been
the combination of these, he was convinced, which had
put him on the way to wealth. His forebears had endowed him with a resolve to succeed and a genius at
using wood and iron. With these he had built wagons.
Came the Civil War, and an immediate demand for
wagons, hundreds of wagons, for the Army of the Po-
tomac. Republican connections in Washington secured
him a contract for their production which doubled,
then tripled, the size of his works and the number of
his employees. Finally, after Appomattox, when fierce

competition almost pushed him to the wall, it had been
the suggestion of his brother, Josephus, to shift from
the manufacture of wagons to sleighs, or cutters. To
this he made no response, but soon made another decision. Within ten years the Cadbury Cutter was the
best-known, largest-selling line of horse-drawn two- and
four-seater cutters in the United States. Now, as the
century drew to a close, the cutter works employed
nearly three hundred people, and its payroll had turned
the small town of Gilead into one of the most prosperous in the state. And as he thumped about amongst his
cats in the wee dark hours, Lycurgus Cadbury reflected
on his accomplishment. Childless he might have been;
he might have lost his wife, Maude, along the way; but
there was this recompense: he was rich beyond his
highest expectations. And he owed it all to blood, family, hard work, and the GOP—and something else. The
will of the Almighty had been done.

He sent a thank-you to the nation once each year, in
December. He thought of it as a Christmas card. He
paid for an entire page in every major newspaper in
the East and Middle West, and ordered set in the center in headline type framed with holly leaves and ber-
ries the following stanza:

> *Jingle bells, jingle bells,*
> *Hearts are all a-flutter.*
> *Oh, what fun it is to ride,*
> *In a fine Cadbury cutter!*

Hetta Mae made haste indeed, arriving at the mansion before ten the next morning. Eli stabled her hired

horse and rig, Josh took her single bag upstairs, and Miss Cadbury was ushered at once into the room off the parlor. She stood at the foot of the bed. She stared. Her uncle opened an eye.

She saw against the pillows and under a nightcap a gray, thin face stubbled with gray beard, lips almost blue, and one dim eye in a deep socket.

He saw a drab woman wearing steel-rimmed spectacles, a black wool suit and white cotton shirtwaist, with mousy hair drawn into a bun and a face pinched up either to start tears or to stay them.

"Uncle—" she breathed.

"Hetty," he sighed. "Already in black, I see."

"But they told me you—"

"That's right. A gone goose."

She commenced to weep, and he closed the eye. A bony hand beckoned her to him. She seated herself on the side of the bed. To certain ladies of middle age, who have sat at many a deathbed and attended many a funeral, the shedding of tears becomes an art rather than an act of mourning. Rather than expressing sorrow, it expresses the artist.

"Now don't faint on me," he warned.

"Are you in pain?"

"No."

"It was a stroke?"

"Yes."

"What does the doctor say?"

He shook his head.

"But people sometimes recover from—"

"No. I don't have long, I can tell."

"Oh, Lycurgus, if you go, what will become of me?"

she wept. "I can scarcely get by now—I scrimp and make do—but if you leave me alone, and Lillian has her way—"

His hand interrupted, took one of hers, indicating he wanted her nearer. She bent to hear his feeble words.

"That's—that's what I want to say to you, Hetty. I've been unfair. I apologize; I must make my peace. You come see me every month—she bothers once a year. And she spends my money as if it grows on trees."

"Wasteful!" agreed Hetta Mae.

"So I'll make it up to you now. I'll give her ample to live on—but I'll leave most of it to you, Hetty. You'll be rich."

"Oh, Lycurgus!" She straightened, drew a cotton hanky, and blew her nose with gladness. "'God moves in a mysterious way His wonders to perform'! You dear, dear—"

She stopped. His hand gripped hers again, with surprising strength.

"You must do a favor for me, Hetty. I beg you."

"Anything, Uncle!"

"See they don't—bury me alive!"

"Alive!" She was horrified. "Oh, my goodness, no! Why in the world would you think—"

But he had released her, and fallen back as though into his last sleep. She watched him. Only his hands moved, the fingers plucking at the edge of the coverlet. She had observed again and again this phenomenon, the fingers plucking, to be the one sure sign that the end was near. Hetta Mae put away her hanky, bowed

her head, and said a silent prayer for his generous soul.
Then she smiled.

Lillian Morgan was as good as her word, reaching
the mansion at noon in the company of six valises, four
hatboxes, and her dearly beloved Montfort, who was
sixteen now and who, since his last visit to Gilead a
year ago, had sprouted up to be taller than his mother.
It was an entrance as much as an arrival. While ordering lunch of Mrs. Pumpley and directing Eli and Josh
upstairs with the luggage and specifying which bedrooms she and Montfort were to occupy, Mrs. Morgan
removed a brown beaver coat to display a tucked pon-
gee shirtwaist to which a small gold watch was pinned,
a brown wool skirt with black stripes, and kid shoes
laced to the calf—this traveling costume topped by a
brown felt hat with a dashingly angled pheasant
feather. Mother and son then made a beeline for the
room off the parlor.

They looked at each other. Lycurgus Cadbury
seemed to be asleep or dead. Lillian Morgan was full-
faced and full-bodied, and carried herself regally, and
would have been altogether attractive had it not been
for a nose too Roman and a voice too loud. Her hair
was always marcelled, and tinted with henna. They
looked again at the man in the bed, and Lillian
stepped forward, perhaps to touch his hand to determine if it was cold. Her rustle roused him. His eyes
opened. In a movement as awkward as it was theatrical
she fell at once to her knees beside him. But she fell too

far—so close to him that the tip of the pheasant
feather on her hat was thrust up his nose. He splut-
tered, and had a coughing fit, and it was some time before he could protest.

"Faugh! Trying to kill me? Get that damned thing
out of my face!"

Lillian made profuse apologies, and removed the hat
while Montfort almost burst to keep from laughter.

"Uncle Ly, I'm so sorry!"

"And get that damned young stinkpot out of here!"

Lillian was aghast. "You don't mean Monty? Why,
he worships the ground you walk on!"

Her offspring puckered his face into an appropriate
mingling of affection and grief.

"He'll worship the ground I'm laid in," growled the
octogenarian. "Away with him!"

His mother gestured, and biting a lip Montfort took
his leave. Mrs. Morgan hoisted herself from the floor,
and seated herself on the bed at a safe distance.

"You're not as ill as I thought," she reproached.

"Not ill enough, hey?"

"I didn't mean that. I merely—"

"Well, I'm done for," Lycurgus insisted. "Hopkins
told me this morning."

"What?"

He turned his face to the wall. "I won't last the
night."

"Ohhh!" His niece put her hands to her brow. "Oh,
Uncle Ly!" And then, as though on cue, a tear appeared in each of her eyes, and trickled in perfect
unison down each of her cheeks. She rocked herself.

"What will become of us? Montfort will soon need college—I shall have to give up my flat—shall I take in laundry? Shall I sell my body in the streets?"

"Turn 'em off, Lil," he said, confronting her.

"Turn what off?"

"The waterworks. There's something I'd better say. I know you require more than Hetty, so—"

"I certainly do. She—an old maid, with neither chick nor child, and—"

"So that's how I've arranged it."

Her interest was instant. "How?"

"Hetty will have enough. She doesn't need much. The bulk of it will go to you."

If he meant what he seemed to mean, it was too good to be true. "Are you saying—"

"Lil, you'll be rich."

Her eyes glittered. Her bosom heaved. "Uncle! Dear, dear Uncle Ly!" Impulsively she smothered him, and kissed his brow, overwhelming him with her perfume.

"Faugh! Leave me be!" With surprising strength he pushed her away. "Never mind that. Lil, there's something you must do for me."

"Anything, Uncle!"

"Don't let them—bury me alive!"

"What!"

"It happens, often. I've read it in the papers. And the thought of it—"

"Don't be absurd." She smiled. "Dear Uncle, nothing like that could—"

But he had turned his face from her again, to the wall, ending the interview. Lillian Morgan had read somewhere, possibly in a novel, that this phenomenon, the turning away to the wall, was the one sure sign of impending death. She sat for a moment, watching him, then rose quietly and stepped to a mirror, resettled her hat fashionably on her head, fixed her face in a mournful mask, and made her exit.

The staff was meanwhile harried and harassed. There were valises to be unpacked, fires to be laid and lit in three bedrooms, a round of beef to be roasted for lunch, an extra horse to be stabled, curried, and fed, and various crises to be met and overcome.

Miss Cadbury's room was too hot for her comfort; Mrs. Morgan's, too cold.

The roast had been ordered too late, and would be underdone unless Josh kept the range roaring.

Brainerd Peckham, the attorney, arrived to confer with his client, Mr. Cadbury, and departed.

Miss Cadbury lay down for a nap after her journey and was rudely awakened in her corset cover by Eli, who tottered into her room unannounced to report that her hired horse had thrown a shoe.

Bending over a valise laid open on a bed, Verbena was approached from the rear by Montfort. Pinched in a place too personal for these pages, she flew to the kitchen in tears. Mrs. Pumpley, mashing potatoes, gave the girl short shrift.

"That'll teach you, missy. Never turn your back on a man, young or old."

"If he lays a hand on her again, I'll thrash him," vowed Josh.

"You do that," warned the housekeeper, "and his mother'll have your scalp."

"I don't care," was the stout rejoinder. "I'll knock him up to a peak and knock the peak off."

"Why ain't it snowed?" demanded Eli.

Doctor Hopkins came a second time that day, examined his patient, entered into a discussion with the nieces, then betook himself to the kitchen—something he had never done. "I regret to say," he told the four, "that in all probability your employer will not last the night. His mind is clear, however, and he has given instructions both to me and to Mr. Peckham. He wishes the funeral to be private—family and servants only—and prefers it to be as soon as feasible after his demise. So ready yourselves; it may be tomorrow. Mr. Teeple, the undertaker, has been put on notice. Oh yes, you are asked to assemble in the parlor at four this afternoon."

"Assemble? What for?" asked Mrs. Pumpley.

Silas Hopkins looked at each in turn. "He wishes you to see the coffin."

Minnie Pumpley went white as her mashed potatoes.

Eli groaned.

Josh gaped.

Verbena gasped. "The coffin!"

They assembled at four, relatives and servants, the former disposed about the great parlor in attitudes of dread and distaste, the latter standing in a fidgety row behind them. Soon the door of Mr. Cadbury's room opened, and through it was rolled upon a four-wheeled carriage a huge coffin of bronze with ornate gilded handles and fittings. The roller was Mr. Teeple, who stopped it at stage center of the room, closed the door behind him, grinned at his audience, and produced a sound remarkably like a chuckle—which in fact it was.

To say the least, Timothy Teeple was an unlikely undertaker. Given his presence and attire, one would have thought him a traveling drummer, or P. T. Barnum brought back to earth. He was bald and rotund, his chin shaven smooth as an apple. He favored checked suits and shirts of striped percale, polka-dot cravats and pearl-gray spats, diamond stickpins, and across his vest on a silver chain, the tooth of an elk. Even worse for one of his profession, he was by nature jolly. Something there was in him which chuckled at eternity, which made jokes about the Grim Reaper, which forced him against his will to keep a straight face at funerals. Nevertheless, despite these shortcomings, he was highly regarded by the citizens of Gilead. He was diligent, he was considerate, he came promptly at any hour in any season, and with every smile he allayed the grief and lightened the burdens of the bereaved.

"Now, ladies and gentlemen," he said, "this is Mr. Cadbury's coffin. I've just shown it to him, and he approves. And he thought you better see it, too, so that when you see it at the service you won't wonder."

Timothy Teeple paused. "Please ask any questions you have as I go along, and I'll explain. First off, you may know that Mr. Cadbury worries about being prematurely buried—that is, before he's dead. It's happened too many times, as we read in the papers. And we none of us would like that, would we?"

He noted the shakings of heads, and continued. "Lots of folks, for years now, have had the same worry—in the U.S. of A. and over in England. So inventors have invented some devices—I call 'em gadgets—that'll make sure that if deceased is buried before he's deceased, he can let it be known and be dug up and saved. Mr. Cadbury has bought the very best of these gadgets, or devices if you will, and what I want to do on this sad occasion is demonstrate 'em to you." He chuckled. "After all, you might be in the market someday yourselves."

His amusement was not shared. He flushed slightly and returned to his subject, pointing to a metal tube, flared and curved at the end, which protruded from the lid of the casket. "This looks like a speaking tube, don't it? Well, that's what it is. If deceased should come to, he can holler through this tube for help. Now, if he's buried underground, we run a length of pipe up from the tube to aboveground, but since Mr. Cadbury will be in the family vault, beside his wife, who I had the pleasure of serving as well, this is all that's needed."

He pointed next at a brass bell mounted on the lid near the speaking tube. "This is known as a 'Bateson's Belfry.' Very popular in England and catching on very well on this side of the pond, I'm glad to say. See this cord? It runs down through a hole in the lid and hangs near deceased's hand. If he changes his mind about shuffling off this mortal coil, he can pull the cord and ring the bell. Oh, it's a crackerjack—guaranteed 100 per cent. Listen to this."

Mr. Teeple raised the lid, inserted an arm, took hold of the cord, and gave the Bateson's Belfry several clangs loud enough to summon a fire company. At the noise, deafening and horrid, Miss Cadbury and Mrs. Morgan covered their ears and exclaimed, Montfort laughed, and the four servants shuddered visibly.

"Mr. Teeple, please spare us!" cried Miss Cadbury.

He bowed. "Your pardon, ma'am. Sorry, ladies, I didn't intend—when I've got a good product, I get carried away sometimes. Now, last but not least," he resumed. "For this I'll need an assistant." He glanced at Josh and smiled. "Josh, is it?"

"Yes, sir."

"Fine. Just step right up here, lad."

Josh did as bade.

The undertaker opened wide the coffin lid, revealing an interior padded and lined with the finest purple satin. "Just put a foot on the carriage, my boy, and I'll lend you a hand."

Josh was hesitant. "I'm to get in, sir?"

"Yes, yes, of course. Here we go."

And with a lift from Mr. Teeple, the reluctant youth clambered into the great receptacle. "Lay right down; make yourself at home."

Josh stretched out prone, his body stiff as a board.

"Now I'll close the lid. Don't be upset. It'll be just a jiffy."

"But, s-s-sir," Josh quavered, "do you have to?"

"Indeed I do. Don't be alarmed, lad, relax." The undertaker lowered the heavy lid, and turned to the gathering with a chuckle. "Can't say as I blame him. Now, ladies and gentlemen, this coffin is spring-loaded. By that I mean parts of it are connected to springs that are wound up tight. Now suppose deceased is laid to rest in a vault. Suppose after a while deceased finds he is not deceased, but fit as a fiddle. Suppose it's night-time, and he hollers through the tube and rings the bell, and nobody hears. What is the poor soul to do?"

Having often rehearsed this exhibition, and having his audience in the palm of his hand by now, Timothy Teeple lowered his voice so that they must strain ears to attend him. One could have heard a pin drop in the parlor. "Back here, on the other side of the coffin, is a little lever." He slipped an arm round a corner of the casket. "The lever works from outside or in—right near deceased's hand." He braced himself. "Now I trip the lever and—presto!"

The lid of the coffin flew open with a thud!

The bottom of the coffin rose with a whir, elevating young Josh to the top with a force that almost cat-apulted him out and onto the floor!

And these occurrences took place so suddenly and with such a clang and clatter of springs that the room was thrown into pandemonium.

Eli Stamp would have keeled over had Verbena not seized him.

Minnie Pumpley fell back against a wall.

Montfort leaped to his feet.

Mrs. Morgan screeched.

Hetta Mae Cadbury fainted dead away.

Shortly after dinner that evening Mrs. Pumpley came to the kitchen, took Josh aside, and ordered him to Mr.

Cadbury's room. She had been there, offering to spoon him some gruel, but he was too weak to eat. "He's failing fast," she said in the boy's ear. "He wants to see you."

"Me? Why?"

"Go."

Josh went directly. Except for a single lamp, and a tongue or two of fire in the fireplace, the library-bedroom-sitting room was dark. He approached the bed.

"Mr. Cadbury?"

He came closer.

"Mr. Cadbury?"

A hand touched his, a cold hand, and taking it drew him down to a face he could but dimly perceive. A toothless mouth opened, and from it came a whisper.

"Josh?"

"Yes, sir."

"I'll—I'll die this night."

"Oh, sir, I hope not."

The cold hand clutched the warm. "After I'm gone, you'll—have to do things for me—brave things. Good boy. Will you—do them?"

"Oh yes, sir."

"Promise."

"I promise."

"And when you do—you'll—be richly rewarded. D'you understand? Richly?"

"I guess so, sir."

The cold hand dropped away. "Richly. Good-by, boy."

Josh let the cats in for the night and went down into the basement to bank the furnace. He was shoveling ashes up from the pit and through the door and over the hot coals when Verbena slipped down the steps.

"I heard Mrs. Pumpley tell you," she said. "What did he want?"

Josh stood the shovel against the grate handle. "He said after he dies, I'll have to do brave things for him."

"What things?"

"I don't know. He made me promise I would."

"Brave things?"

"He said if I do, I'll be richly rewarded. He said 'richly' three times."

"Three times? Oh, Josh!"

They stood together under a bare light bulb. The furnace hissed and sputtered at them. Verbena's eyes were bright with hope.

"I'm not even going to think about it," Josh said stubbornly. "After all, there's Miss Cadbury and Mrs. Morgan and Montfort."

"He doesn't care a fig for them."

"Even so, they're his relatives. He wouldn't—"

"He might!"

*"I will now inject a solution of strychnine."*

# 3

# "Testis Unus, Testis Nullus"

ad they known what the ensuing hours held in store for them, it is doubtful those resident in the mansion would have sought a sweet repose that night at all. Seek it they did, however, guests and servants alike—one of them unsuccessfully. Dreaming of the Wild West, Joshua Overland was waked at midnight by a hand clapped roughly over his mouth. He struggled, but in vain, and as his eyes adjusted to the darkness, he recognized his assailant as none other than Dr. Hopkins, who ordered him to be silent, and to come downstairs at once. The youth did so, and in the kitchen was directed without further explanation to accompany the physician. They passed through the dining room and the great parlor, stumbling over several cats

in their progress, then through the door of Mr. Cadbury's room. The door was closed behind them by someone. Josh turned to determine who.

"Joshua, isn't it?"

"Yes, sir."

"I am Brainerd Peckham."

"I know, sir."

Silas Hopkins laid a hand on Josh's shoulder. "You should be told, Josh, why I have brought you here. Your employer is in intolerable pain. He has begged me, as a friend, to do him one last kindness—to put him out of his misery. I have consented. He is near the end in any case, and there is nothing more I can do for him—except this. Do you understand?"

"Yes, sir. No, sir."

"You must be a witness."

"Witness?"

"To what I am about to do. To observe it, and to give testimony under oath if need be."

"But, sir, why—why me?"

The attorney spoke. " '*Testis unus, testis nullus.*' It is a legal maxim which, translated from the Latin, means 'A single witness is no witness.' To an act, that is, in a court of law. In short, I cannot be the sole witness to what the doctor intends. There must be a second. And you shall serve in that capacity."

Josh stared at him, the recognition of what was about to transpire, and the weight of the responsibility he was about to assume, bearing more heavily upon his shoulders than the doctor's hand. Brainerd Peckham was a tall man, sallow of complexion, skeletal of frame, a man in his sixties whose black serge suits and stern features and sparse hair and spade beard shot with gray and old-fashioned celluloid collars made him a formidable, even an ominous, figure. None of the servants had ever known him to smile. Verbena had appraised him an ideal candidate, she said, to "haunt a house." And staring at him, a chore boy of fourteen in a union suit, Josh shivered with much more than cold.

"Oh, sir," he implored, "do I have to?"

Peckham knit his brows. "Did Mr. Cadbury not ask you this evening to do him certain favors? Did you not promise him you would?"

"Yes, sir. But—"

"I assure you this is but the first, and the easiest."

"But, sir, I didn't think that—"

"We will hear no more. Hopkins, let us have it over and done with."

"Very well." The doctor closed the velvet drapes, removed his coat, and rolled his shirt sleeves to the elbows. "I need more light." He stepped into the adjoining bathroom, turned a switch, and while there washed his hands scrupulously. Leaving the bathroom door ajar, upon return he placed his black bag on the bed and opened it. "Will you two please stand on the far side of the bed?"

The two witnesses took their places. Mr. Cadbury appeared to be asleep or unconscious.

Hopkins brought forth from the bag a hypodermic syringe equipped with a plunger at one end and a long needle at the other. "I do not need to swear you to secrecy, do I, Josh?" he asked. "Or do I?"

"You had better," advised the attorney.

Hopkins nodded. "Perhaps. Josh, you must swear by your God and on your honor never to divulge what you have seen and heard in this room tonight—unless and until you are released from your oath. Do you so swear?"

"I guess so, sir."

"Say it."

"I swear."

"Very well. I will now inject a solution of strychnine. Death will be painless, and should occur, if I have calculated correctly, within two minutes. What is the time, Brainerd?"

The attorney slipped a turnip of a gold watch from a vest pocket, opened the case, and squinted. "It is eight minutes past midnight. This, then, is the first day of December."

Holding the syringe in his right hand, with his left Silas Hopkins turned down the coverlet, found a thin arm, and raised it so that the nightshirt sleeve slid down to expose the inner surface of the elbow. He bent low, and moved the arm into the shaft of light from the bathroom. He searched for a large vein into which to inject the strychnine. He located one. He poised the needle.

A clawing at the door startled men and boy. It was a cat, or more than one. Were Mr. Cadbury's pets aware of what was being done to their friend and benefactor?

Joshua Overland had a look around the gloomy room—at the maw of the fireplace, at the muffles of the drapes, at the glass-fronted bookcases shelved with leather volumes, at the busts of Homer and Virgil, Browning and Lord Tennyson, atop the cases, at the ornate mahogany desk shoved against a wall, then at the matchstick of an arm, the long steel needle nearing a vein. He had never himself been inoculated. He had never seen anyone injected. He had never before been in the presence of death. He had never before seen a human being killed. Against such horror, incredible and indescribable, he shut his eyes tightly.

"Open your eyes, boy."

It was the grim voice of the attorney.

Josh opened them.

He witnessed a needle inserted deep into white and living flesh.

He witnessed a thumb depress a plunger, and the slow transfer of dark fluid, of poison, from syringe into bloodstream.

He witnessed the two men wait, the elder intent on the face of his watch. He heard the ticking of the watch.

"Two minutes," intoned the attorney.

Silas Hopkins bent again, and laid a hand on what only two minutes ago had been the beating heart of Lycurgus Harold Cadbury.

"He's gone," he murmured.

Brainerd Peckham cleared his throat and put away his watch. "Let us pray," he said. "Let us ask forgiveness of Almighty God."

There was more to come before the dawn—much more.

Shortly after one o'clock Dr. Hopkins turned on the twin chandeliers in the great parlor, awakened the household, and when relatives and servants were collected, informed them with regret that Lycurgus Cadbury had but minutes before departed this earth. The passing had been peaceful, he was glad to state, and he had already telephoned Mr. Teeple.

Minnie Pumpley burst into tears, as did Verbena out of empathy. It was the nieces, however, who put on the better display. Hetta Mae Cadbury and Lillian Morgan each fell into the other's arms and wept copiously upon the other's robe—Hetta Mae's of muslin, Lillian's of silk trimmed with velvet.

"Uncle, Uncle!" wailed Miss Cadbury. "That great man, that generous man!"

"Dear Uncle Ly!" wailed Mrs. Morgan. "Gone, gone forever!"

"Oh, Lillian!" wailed Hetta Mae. "What will you do without him?"

"Hetty, Hetty!" wailed Lillian. "What will you do without him?"

Their selflessness was good to see. It had been noted in the kitchen how cordial to each other they were after each was closeted alone with her uncle that afternoon. It could not be known of course that both had been promised by him the bulk of his estate—reason enough for each woman to be gracious to the other. Now their common loss seemed to make them sisters again, and their relationship sincere and loving rather than merely familial. Leaning upon each other and leaving a trail of tears, they ascended the stairs, escorted by a silent Montfort as stricken by grief no doubt as they.

There was no rest for the staff. In half an hour Mr. Teeple rang the bell, with a helper, and the body of the deceased was removed from the house by stretcher. The undertaker returned then and informed them that the funeral would take place this very day, at three in the afternoon, in the chapel of the church.

"Today!" protested Mrs. Pumpley.

"Today, ma'am," was the reply. "I know it's sudden, but those were Mr. Cadbury's instructions. And it's to be private."

"But the works—the folks at the cutter works."

"Not even a minute of silence. They are to stay on the job."

"On his dying day?"

"His very words. The service will be for family only, plus Dr. Hopkins, Mr. Peckham, and you four."

She sighed. "We'll have to make the best of it. But the ladies upstairs'll have conniptions."

"That may be, ma'am, but they'll be there like the coffin." Timothy Teeple chuckled. "With bells on."

He left them. They withdrew to the kitchen. Mrs. Pumpley declared for cocoa again, and while Verbena heated milk, she prepared the syrup.

"Today," she grumped.

"Master knowed, so he was ready." Eli nodded sagely, tightening the sock about his neck. "I recollect the Wilderness. We knowed, too, when the battle come the next day, we'd be goners, every man jack of us. Know what we done? Writ our names on papers, and where we

wanted buried, and pinned 'em on our backs. Down in
Virginny that was."

"Will I have to go home tomorrow night?" asked
Verbena of the housekeeper. "I mean, tonight?"

This conversation irked Josh, who sat on a stool biting his tongue. Going home, old wars, funeral times—
these were insignificant subjects compared to the scene
he had witnessed tonight. Had he not been sworn to secrecy, he would certainly have poured it out to them—
the syringe, the poison, Mr. Peckham's presence; indeed, he was on the very verge, and might have had he
not been prevented by Lillian Morgan, who sailed unexpectedly into the kitchen in silken robe and hair net.

"You're unduly noisy, all of you," she asserted. "I am
unable to sleep. Now hush, this instant, and off to bed
—" She frowned. Verbena at the range, Mrs. Pumpley
with spoon and saucepan, caught her attention. "Why,
what are you doing? Mrs. Pumpley?"

"Making cocoa, mum," responded the housekeeper
with a tinge of defiance. "We're all so frazzled out—"

"Cocoa!"

As though it were her name, Hetta Mae Cadbury
appeared in somewhat bedraggled condition. "All this
to-do—I haven't slept a wink! I've had to take something for my nerves. I've—"

"Hetty, you can't imagine!" cried Mrs. Morgan.
"They're making cocoa!"

"Cocoa!"

"Without permission! Uncle Ly scarcely out of the
house and they—"

"Well, I never!" cried Miss Cadbury. "The gall!"

Mrs. Morgan swept the room with eyes like artillery. "You'll stop this instant, and there'll be no more sneaking about and wasting foodstuffs. My sister and I have charge of this house now, and we'll give orders. Will we not, Hetty?"

"Indeed we will, Lillian. Is that clear, Mrs. Pumpley?" snapped the spinster.

The housekeeper glowered into her saucepan. "Yes, mum," she said.

Both sisters sniffed; then heads high in righteous triumph, they twined arms and betook themselves to bed again, as did the servants.

It was not to be for long. A little past three o'clock in the morning everyone in the mansion was snatched abruptly from the arms of Morpheus by a scream. It emanated from the servants' quarters, from Verbena's bedroom to be specific. Instead of first, Josh was last to rush to her rescue, for in rising hastily from his tick he cracked his head against the ceiling of his cubbyhole, fell back, and lay dizzied for a minute or two before he could regain balance enough to crawl out and down the hall.

Miss Cadbury and Mrs. Morgan had just reached Verbena's door, having entered the quarters through the door which connected with the guest bedrooms on the second floor. Old Eli tottered from his room, and Mrs. Pumpley puffed from hers.

Suddenly, from out of the maid's room, walked Montfort Morgan in a nightshirt, his steps slow and measured, his eyes closed, both arms stiff and extended before him. He passed Josh, opened an eye, winked, then proceeded through the connecting door in the direction of his own room.

Verbena herself appeared, almost hysterical.

"What happened, girl?" demanded Mrs. Pumpley.

"He—he came in my room!" sobbed the child. "I was never so scared! What did he want?"

"Ridiculous!" Lillian Morgan drew herself up and folded her arms. "He was just sleepwalking. He often does."

"No, he wasn't!" Verbena bawled.

"Flibbertigibbet," scoffed Hetta Mae. "Montfort is a perfect gentleman."

"No, he isn't! He tried to get in my bed!"

"Hussy!" cried Mrs. Morgan. "My son interested in a kitchen drudge? I'll not listen to another word! Come, Hetty."

The sisters stalked away to their rooms, after which it took no little time to calm Verbena, and to tuck her in again. And she was settled down in the end only by Josh's offer to bring his blanket into the hall, lie down on the floor, and stand guard at her door for the remainder of the night.

The worst of it, alas, was yet to be. An hour or so later, after four o'clock, there rose from the parlor into the guest rooms and the servants' quarters a loud and hideous chorus. It was the cats. It was as though the animals had only then come to the conclusion that their friend, their protector, was lost in truth to them forever, and had decided to mourn him in song. The sound they made had everyone up in seconds, and downstairs into the parlor soon thereafter. Taking a cat

count now was easy. Seventeen of them, tom and female, fat and lean, sleek and mangy, black and gray
and white and orange and every hodgepodge of these,
were ranged before the door of Lycurgus Cadbury's
room, their heads tilted back, and from their throats issued a collective caterwauling which split the ears.

"Get them out, get them out!" cried Mrs. Morgan,
covering hers.

Miss Cadbury could not believe hers. "Lillian, how
could you? You know Lycurgus loved them. He'd turn
over in his grave if we—"

"I don't care if he spins like a top!" Mrs. Morgan
thrust an arm at Eli and Josh. "Take them away!"

"Throw 'em in the fireplace and burn 'em up, I
say," offered Montfort.

Miss Cadbury thrust an arm at Eli and Josh. "Don't
touch them. My dear uncle—"

"Dear uncle, my foot!" cried her sister. "He's gone
and we're here! And if you won't allow me to sleep,
Hetty, I shall go to the grave with him! That's what
you want, isn't it? Then you'd have it all, wouldn't
you?"

The language, and the accusation, took Miss Hetta
Mae aback. She steadied herself with a hand on a sofa;
she looked as though she might weep, and have need of
a hanky, or swoon again, and have need of smelling
salts. But if there was weakness in her posture, there
was starch in her spinster spine. She recovered herself.
She drew her robe about her.

"Very well, Lillian," she said with dignity. "Do as
you wish—this time."

And so it fell to old Eli and Josh to undertake the removal of the animals. They put on shoes and hats and coats. A cat under each arm, they marched back and forth from house to stable. Mr. Cadbury had never permitted his pets to roam at night, and in deference to this the animals were put in the granary, a room within the stable lined with grain bins and piled with hay, and the door shut upon all seventeen of them. Here they would be sheltered and safe from harm until release in the morning. When they had finished, Josh had to help Eli up the back porch steps, and once through the storm door, the aged veteran leaned against a wall, short of breath.

"I be tuckered. That Montfort—ain't he a rip?"

"I hate him," Josh muttered.

"Them women. They'll come to scratch and claw yet, you'll see."

"I s'pose they will."

"We be in for a fracas. Turrible fracas." Eli Stamp gripped both of Josh's arms, and fixed him with a rheumy eye. "Buryin' today. I got no place to go after. Poor farm? You got a place, boy?"

"No."

"Why don't it snow?"

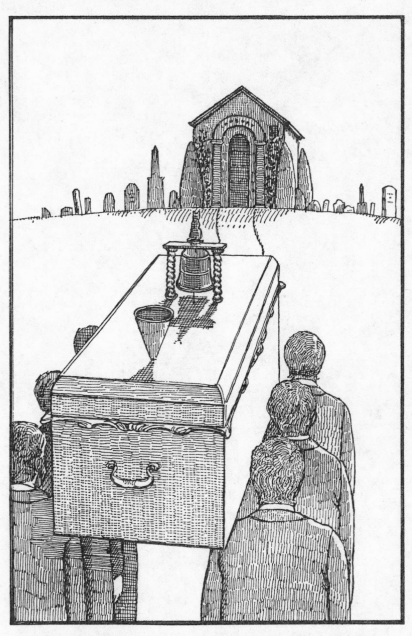

*"'Earth to earth, ashes to ashes, dust to dust . . .'"*

# 4

# "Ashes to Ashes, Dust to Dust"

 top!"

Josh ran as swiftly as his legs would take him.

"Stop!"

Air whistled into and out of his lungs as he shouted.

It had been midmorning before he found a spare moment to free the cats imprisoned in the stable. To be certain he let go all seventeen, he stood by the door as they came out, purring and rubbing his legs—but he tallied only thirteen. He searched the granary, looking into each bin, clambering over hay bales. Perplexed, he went out into the yard to see if he could account for the missing four, and glanced by chance to the south. There, some two hundred yards from the mansion, lay

the Deerkill River, a deep though narrow stream which
flowed westward and drained, eventually, into the
mighty Hudson.

"Stop!"

Nearing the bridge, Josh knew, no matter how fast
he ran, that he would be too late to prevent the despicable deed. For there on the bridge, wearing a bowler
hat and a flannel suit with silver buttons and a bow tie
and brilliant yellow shoes, Montfort Morgan revolved,
swinging round and round a weighted gunnysack.

"Stop!"

Josh reached the bridge, slowed, and reached its center just as Montfort let the gunnysack fly out over the
Deerkill and fall with a splash into the stream.

It was Josh who stopped and stared, sickened, over
the side. Usually a fine place for ice skating by now,
the river this year, due to the unusually mild weather,
had not yet frozen over. The sack, which seemed to
move for a moment on the surface as though it were
alive, sank slowly out of sight into a watery grave.

Montfort smirked at him. "There, that's four of 'em.
I couldn't find another sack or I'd have eight."

Josh clenched his fists—but behind his back. Young
Mr. Morgan was two years older and, although slight
of physique, a head taller, and his station in life was so
exalted compared to that of a chore boy that there was
really no comparison at all. "That was—an awful
trick!" Josh puffed. "Don't you dare—drown any
more!"

"Who says?"

"I do!"

"What'll you do about it, clodhopper?"

"I'll—I'll thrash you!"

Montfort laughed without humor. "Ha. Ha. You and who else? I'll have you know I've been trained in the manly art of self-defense."

"Those cats are Mr. Cadbury's," Josh reminded.

"Were, you mean. The old goat's gone—finally," sneered Montfort. "My mother's getting most of the estate—he told her so. So as soon as the will's read, I'm hauling the damned cats down here one by one by the tails and pitching 'em in." He cocked his bowler hat at a Broadway angle. "And you can put that in your pipe and smoke it." He shoved hands into pockets, remarked, "It's colder than billy hell," and started with long strides for the mansion.

Josh followed, trying to keep pace, repelled by the city youth yet at the same time fascinated. Montfort's face was pinched and mean, his eyes an insipid and wary blue. His upper lip sported several sandy hairs, and these he rubbed every day with bicycle oil, which he had heard would produce a mustache faster than one could say "Jack Robinson."

"You worked for the old bugger—how rich was he?" he inquired.

"How should I know?" retorted Josh.

"Well, I know one thing. He was tighter than the paper on the wall. And he could have been a lot richer. Cutters—ye gods. They're going out with the horse and buggy. Guess what Ma and I are going to do as soon as we get our hands on the cutter works. Shut it down. Guess what we're going to make instead."

Montfort pulled his bow tie out from his collar by its elastic band and let it thwack back into place. "Autos!"

"Autos?"

"Automobiles! That's the future, dummy."

"It is?"

"Sure! Don't you hicks read the papers up here in the sticks? The streets in New York are full of 'em—Duryeas, Locomobiles, Wintons, Columbias—and a brand-new baby, the Stanley Steamer. Runs on steam, goes like a house afire!"

Josh had never heard such tommyrot. He swallowed little of it. His companion was a snob and a swell, a braggart and a dastard and assuredly a liar, but assuredly he gave one an earful, and so when Montfort attained the dried brown lawns of the mansion and detoured behind the stable, Josh tagged along.

Montfort slipped a small flat can from a pocket, opened it, and offered. "Here. Want some snuff?"

"Snuff?"

"Tobacco, only ground up fine."

"No, thank you."

"Suit yourself." Montfort pinched some between thumb and forefinger, opened his mouth, and stuffed it between cheek and gum. "Copenhagen, the best. I don't go for cigars, and chewing a cud of tobacco is farmerish. Give me snuff and a cuspidor and shut the door."

Josh wanted to put a question, but did not know how to go about it. "What'll—I mean—if your ma gets all you say—what'll she do?"

"I told you. Cut the cutters and start the autos. And sell this barn of a house. We'll live in the city."

"What about us?"

"Who?"

"Well, Mrs. Pumpley and Eli."

"Sack 'em."

"But, but they're old, and they don't have anyplace to—"

"That's the trouble. They're practically pushing up daisies now, and old Stamp's nuttier than a fruitcake. So out they go, into the cold, boo-hoo." Montfort spat a splendid spit on the stable wall.

"What about—what about Verbena and me?"

"You? Buy a monkey and beg." Montfort reconsidered. "Maybe not Verbena, though. Maybe I'll talk Ma into taking her to New York with us."

Josh scowled. "Why?"

"Why not?" Montfort snapped his fingers. "I'll bet she wears a peach of a pair of bloomers!"

The last rites for Lycurgus Harold Cadbury were held promptly at three o'clock that afternoon in the small, austere chapel off the nave of the tycoon's church. The coffin was open, and placed in state on a pedestal behind the Reverend George Fothergill, who officiated. The mourners could just see the profile of the corpse, its head pillowed on purple satin. Timothy Teeple, the undertaker, had been responsible for the arrangements, and had followed Mr. Cadbury's instructions to the letter. There were no flowers. There would

be no music; the cutter king despised music as much as
he did the other arts. The death notice would not appear in the Gilead newspaper for yet another three
days, since it was a weekly. No announcement had been
sent to metropolitan newspapers. The service was private, with only fourteen in attendance: Mrs. Lillian
Morgan and her son; Miss Hetta Mae Cadbury; Dr.
Silas Hopkins; Mr. Brainerd Peckham; the four servants; Mr. Teeple and three assistants, whose brawn
was required in the handling of the coffin; and of
course Reverend Fothergill. Few tears were shed, although Mrs. Morgan was observed now and then to ca-
ress her nose with a silken hanky. She was costumed in
a style befitting the occasion—a toque hat with satin
crown and bow, and under a coat of black Alaskan seal
a high-necked blouse of lace over a wasp-waisted skirt
of braided black taffeta. Miss Cadbury wore the frugal
black she had worn without respite since her arrival.
Montfort was well-mannered enough to remove his
bowler hat and close his eyes throughout, presumably in
grief. The servants were attired in their dress uniforms.
Mrs. Pumpley's was a shapeless black Mother Hubbard
with a white apron; Verbena's, a black muslin. Josh
wore a thrift-shop ensemble consisting of tweed
knickers, knee socks, and a wool jacket with a Buster
Brown collar. Eli's black suit, smelling of mothballs,
was so old that it had turned a museum green and its
gilt buttons had tarnished. To add a note of patriotism,
he had worn to the church, and held in his lap, the
relic red-peaked, black-billed cap which had long ago
crowned the uniform of the Second New York Zouaves.

Reverend Fothergill's eulogy was brief, again on instructions of the deceased. It began with a biography in broadest outline of Lycurgus Cadbury, and concluded with this short paean of praise: "He is gone from us now, but he cannot be forgotten. A friend to presidents, he was also friend to the good folk of this community. As they gave him wealth, he gave them bread. As they gave him the sweat of their brows, he gave them the security of steady toil. As they gave him their respect, he gave them in return the inspiration of his genius. And so long as a single Cadbury Cutter glides the city streets and country lanes of this land, his name will live." The minister bowed his head. "Let us unite now in prayer for everlasting peace—peace within the tomb for his mortal remains, peace in a higher sphere for his immortal soul."

They prayed.

It was over. The coffin was closed, revealing the speaking tube protruding from the lid and the Bateson's Belfry mounted on it. The mourners filed from the chapel. The coffin was brought down from its pedestal by Mr. Teeple and his assistants, and such was its weight that Dr. Hopkins and Mr. Peckham were pressed into service as pallbearers. The men carried the burden down the aisle and outdoors and laboriously loaded it into the hearse. During the loading it tipped precariously for an instant, causing the bell on its lid to ring and startle all and sundry half out of their skins.

This was another in a succession of drear days. It was cold, yet not cold enough to snow or freeze. Under a lowering sky the funeral cortege made its slow, sad

way toward the town cemetery. The hearse was a
black-roofed van enclosed by glass so that the coffin
was visible inside; it was drawn by two black horses
driven by a coachman in a stovepipe hat high atop a
seat between two brass lamps. Had there been snow,
the mourners would of course have been transported by
cutter, but since the ground was bare, a variety of vehicles was used. Relatives and Reverend Fothergill were
conveyed in a handsome enclosed Brewster calash
coach, driven by Eli Stamp. The other three servants,
Mr. Teeple, and two of his helpers were packed into an
open English phaeton. Hopkins drove his own phaeton,
while Peckham brought up the rear in an enclosed
Rockaway coupe with a driver who doubled as his legal
clerk. Slowly, sadly, the cortege snailed the three blocks
to the clip-clop of hoofs, the tink and squeak of harness, the rumble of iron-rimmed wheels. There was
conversation only in the calash coach, and that only
once.

"If I was running this show," said an impatient
Montfort, "I'd haul him in a Stanley Steamer."

"Shame," said Miss Cadbury.

"Tsk-tsk," chided the minister.

"He's only a boy," apologized Mrs. Morgan.

"I'd fire up the boiler," added her son, "and have
the old skinflint there so fast it'd rattle his bones."

In spring and summer the town cemetery was a
lovely sylvan place, green and hospitable and dappled
with sunlight between the avenues of elms. In fall the
leaves turned color, whispered farewell as they fell, and
were swept up by winds into ricks and drifts of gold.

Even so, it was a place shunned by the children of Gilead as children everywhere incline, calling it "The Bone Yard" or "The Marble Orchard" and making up tales of sights and sounds there too terrible to tell, too horrible to hear. Now, in cheerless December, adults avoided it unless they had no choice. The trees were naked, the shadows melancholy. A thousand dead inhabited it perhaps, most of them beneath humble headstones. A few more prosperous merchants and professional men had erected tall pillars of Vermont granite topped with urns or crosses, or the sculptured figures of maidens modestly draped and gazing heavenward, masterpieces of stonemasonry; and about their columns as the years passed they had gathered wives and sons and daughters under simple markers—reunions of love in stone and death.

But lo, one structure dominated all. It resembled a small house. It had cost a small fortune. It was made of stone and concrete, and roofed with copper. It was built to endure eternity. It was what was known as a "family mausoleum." On three sides windows were inset, of stained Italian glass. On the fourth side, facing the sandy carriage path, was an iron door, and over the door a name in capitals, and under that a carved inscription:

## CADBURY

*Until the Day Break, and the Shadows Flee Away*

Before this tomb the hearse halted, as did the other vehicles. The mourners descended. With a key, Mr.

Peckham unlocked the iron door of the mausoleum.
The coffin was unloaded from the hearse and carried to
the door, where the pallbearers paused while Reverend
Fothergill intoned over it these words:

"'Earth to earth, ashes to ashes, dust to dust; in sure
and certain hope of the Resurrection unto eternal
life.'"

The coffin was borne inside, and after a moment the
pallbearers reappeared. The ceremony was completed,
the last honors done Lycurgus Cadbury. Brainerd Peckham signified that he wished to speak in private with
relatives and servants, and these joined him at a little
distance from the tomb.

"It is my intention to meet with you tomorrow morning at ten o'clock, at the house," he said. "I expect all
to be present."

"To read the will, of course," assumed Mrs. Morgan.

The attorney raised his brows. "That remains to be
seen, does it not, madam?"

She tossed her head.

He put on his Homburg hat. "Eli, Joshua, please
stay after the rest have gone. I have something to say
to you."

The hearse rolled away, as did the calash and phaeton and Dr. Hopkins' covered phaeton. Josh and Eli
waited on the attorney, Josh remarking that the door of
the mausoleum had been left open. Peckham consulted
his watch. Already the day was dying, and a zephyr
caused the limbs of the elm trees high above to trem-
ble.

"What I have to share with you is of the utmost importance," Brainerd Peckham began. "Your employer was a sensible man. He accepted the inevitability of death. He was also a cautious man. He had his coffin fitted out with warning devices, which you have seen demonstrated. He had one fear, you see—not an irrational one among the elderly. He feared being buried alive. And while this is unlikely, it has occurred from time to time, I grant."

"Grant!" exclaimed Eli.

"Grant?"

"Gin'ral U. S. Grant! My old commander!"

Peckham showed some exasperation. "We are not discussing General Grant, Eli, but Mr. Cadbury, and his fear of premature burial. It was his determination that a matter as serious as this should not be left to chance. He therefore gave explicit instructions." He looked straight at the veteran. "Eli, you are to stand guard—I put it in military terms for your sake—in the mausoleum for three days, during daylight hours. This will count as the first day. In other words, for the rest of today, tomorrow, and the day after, you will station yourself near the coffin. Should you hear Mr. Cadbury's voice through the speaking tube, or should he ring the bell, you are to return immediately to the house and see that Dr. Hopkins is notified. Is that clear?"

Eli took off his infantry cap, then put it on again. His face, wrinkled as a prune, worked with an effort at understanding. "But it be cold in there!" he objected. "My lumbago!"

"I am sorry."

Eli fumbled with a tarnished button. "But I'm old!" he quavered. "It be scary here 'mongst the corpses!"

"You have been a soldier," countered the attorney. "You will do your duty, will you not?"

It was an argument Eli could not rebut. "Yes, sir. Duty be my bread and butter."

Peckham turned. "You, Joshua, have the more difficult assignment. As Eli is to keep vigil by day, you shall by night."

"Night!" Josh tried to swallow, but could not. "By night, sir?"

"Exactly. For three nights, this one included. Should the deceased use any of the signaling devices, you are to run at once to Dr. Hopkins' house and so inform him. Is that clear?"

Josh was rendered speechless, and taking his silence for assent, the attorney concluded, "This is to be your employer's margin of safety—three days after death. He felt, and I agree, that should three days pass with nothing untoward happening, he might be considered permanently at rest." He buttoned his overcoat. "Very well. I will give you a lift home, Joshua. Eli, I have left the door open. Joshua will return to relieve you when night falls. Now take your station."

Private Eli Stamp faced the tomb, came to rickety attention, and raised a hand to his cap in salute.

"I'm a-comin', Gin'ral!" he cried, then marched toward the iron door.

On the way to the mansion, Josh sat stiffly in a corner of the enclosed Rockaway coupe. The upholstery was gray, and there were paper flowers in a glass vase attached to a window molding. He saw them not.

"Poor Eli," reflected the attorney aloud. "He gave evidence of senility before this. I hope we have not pushed him over the brink."

So awful, so overwhelming was the prospect which confronted his youthful passenger that he was incapable of thinking about Eli—nay, about anyone except himself. "Three—nights—sir?"

"That is correct," said Brainerd Peckham. "I trust you do not take the position that Mr. Cadbury's order is unreasonable. I assure you it is not. In England, servants are frequently called upon to act as sentry at the gravesite for as long as a month. Surely you would not expect the family to perform such a service?"

"Oh no, sir, not the ladies. But—but what about Montfort? He's older than me, and—"

Peckham shook his head. "You are made of sterner stuff than he, Joshua. Mr. Cadbury was an excellent judge of character."

Josh twisted and turned. He did not care that his knee socks were falling down. He hated to wear knickers when at his age he should be in long trousers, but these had never been provided him.

"But, Mr. Peckham, sir," he said miserably. "A cemetery—a tomb—all by myself—for three nights. I just don't think I can manage—"

"Nonsense. I remind you of your bargain, as I did last night. You promised Mr. Cadbury to do certain favors for him after his death, did you not? And he in return offered to reward you richly, did he not?"

"Yes, sir."

"Then do them."

Poor Josh was placed between the devil and the deep blue sea. He set a cleft chin. "Sir, what—what if I won't?" he made bold to inquire.

The attorney set a bearded jaw. "You must. You cannot say no. You are legally a charge of the state of New York till you are sixteen. If you fail to do as you are told by your employer, to whom you were released, it will go hard with you. Do you wish to go back to the orphanage?"

Josh's heart sank. "Oh no, sir!"

"Then have done with this shilly-shallying." Brainerd Peckham sat back in the seat, satisfied. "You are fortunate."

"F-f-fortunate, sir?" Josh stammered.

"Indeed," was the harsh reply. "How would you like to be asked to monitor the grave for a month?"

They were in the kitchen. Outside, the shades of night drew nigh. Tending first to his chores, Josh had changed into bib overalls, coaled the furnace, fed the six fireplaces, and taken a pan of scraps to the stable for the cats. When he then disclosed to Verbena and Mrs. Pumpley the ordeal to which he and Eli were to be put, they stared at him in disbelief.

"No!" breathed Verbena, rolling her violet eyes. "Oh, goodness, gracious, no!"

"Mercy of God!" whispered the housekeeper. "Three days in a mausoleum—Eli will go dotty!"

"He already has, I guess," said Josh. "He thinks he's guarding General Grant's tomb."

"And three nights!" Mrs. Pumpley rammed a leg of mutton into a roaster. "Nobody, man or boy, should be asked to—"

"I wasn't asked. I was ordered."

"By who?"

"Mr. Peckham."

"There!" Verbena was immediately excited. "That's what Mr. Cadbury meant!"

"Mr. Cadbury?" asked the housekeeper.

"Yes, last night, when he wanted Josh," babbled the little maid. "He said after he died Josh'd have to do brave things, and if he did he'd be richly rewarded. Don't you see, this is what he meant! And maybe if Josh stays three nights, he'll get something in the will! Maybe a lot!"

Mrs. Pumpley frowned. "Hush, girl. Don't either of you get your hopes—"

"It isn't true anyway," said Josh, and revealed what Montfort had revealed to him that morning. "His mother'll get it all. Mr. Cadbury told her so."

Verbena's face fell.

"That's odd—odder than Dick's hat." Mrs. Pumpley forgot to put the top on the roaster. "I was in the small parlor this morning with Miss Hetta Mae, and she said her uncle told her she'd have the most of it. That's what she said."

Verbena puzzled. "You mean, he told each one the same thing? But why—"

"It's only their word," decided the housekeeper. "But if it's true, oh, how the fur'll fly when they find out!" She banged the top on the roaster. "It's neither here nor there nor none of our affair. Josh has got to go this minute. Eli will be cold and hungry."

Josh bolted down an early supper. He donned his woolen jacket and a knitted stocking cap to pull down over his ears. Mrs. Pumpley wound a scarf about his neck, gave him an afghan with which to cover himself, the kitchen stool on which to sit, and Verbena permission to walk with him as far as the cemetery.

They walked briskly, carrying the stool between them. No stars were out, for the night, like the day, was cloudy. They walked without a word. She thought about him. He thought about her. She pitied him, and was frightened for him. He resolved to be brave for her sake, to prove to her that fourteen could be as much a man as sixteen, or even twenty-one. When they reached the entrance to the cemetery, which was but two blocks from the mansion, they put down the stool and Josh slung the afghan over his shoulder. She came close to him.

"Here," she said, and slipped something soft into his hand.

"What is it?"

"Can't you guess?"

"I can't see."

"A lock of my hair."

"Oh, Verbena." He thrust it under his jacket, into

an upper pocket of his overalls. "I've put it near my heart. Gee, thank you."

She came so close to him that even in the darkness he could trace the outline of her face before him like a valentine.

"Oh, Josh," she whispered, "I'm afraid!"

"Don't be, Verbena."

"But I am. For you!"

"I'm not," he assured her.

It was a lie of love.

*He was out the door and running cramped and stiff-legged . . .*

# 5

# The First Night: "Help!"

aden with stool and afghan, he trod the sandy vehicle track into the night. He had entered the cemetery only a few rods when Eli Stamp loomed up, on his way home relief or no relief. Josh asked if everything was all right, but the old man seemed struck dumb, by cold or fear or both, and rushed on past as fast as he was capable, without gesture or utterance.

Joshua Overland was alone. He walked on, alone with the pillars of granite, the crosses and urns, the draped figures of maidens, the headstones and the markers; alone with a wind which moaned and whimpered through the trees' bare branches; alone with a thousand dead.

He came to the mausoleum. The iron door yawned. Putting one leaden foot before the other, he intruded, entering a darkness more Stygian than the dark outside. His footfalls echoed. The floor of the tomb was marble. He stood for a time, listening. There was no sound here, not even the wind, save for the beating of his heart, save for the tide and ebb of air within his lungs. Joshua Overland was more frightened than he had believed a human being could ever be.

"Hello," he whispered, and heard the sibilance repeated.

"Hello," he said. Hello—the greeting was returned to him—hello—off massive stone and concrete walls— hello—and out of corners distant yet nearby—hello.

He forced himself to strain his eyesight, to look about him. He could detect the rectangles of stained glass in three walls, and in the center of the room, something else.

There they were. Side by side, two great coffins sat on marble catafalques, or pedestals, three feet high. On the lid of the one nearer the door he could perceive the speaking tube and Bateson's Belfry. The other, behind it, would be the coffin of his late employer's long-departed spouse. There they lay, Maude and Lycurgus Cadbury; there they would lie forever, bride and groom in bronze, man and wife in silence.

Josh put the stool against a wall, sat down facing the caskets to have support for his back, yoked the afghan about his shoulders, and pulled it tight around him. Sleep was impossible. Since he had left the mansion by six o'clock, it would not be light, Eli would not come, till six in the morning. He must stay here twelve long hours. And if a mere two hours by day in a mausoleum were partially responsible for the loss of Eli's reason, how was he to bear twelve by night without losing his own?

First he tried feeling sorry for himself, but self-pity was foreign to his nature.

He heard the mournful whistle of a train. The line ran up from New York City through Gilead and by spur to Canada, but the main line bent west, toward Pittsburgh and Chicago and thence to prairies, mountains, and adventure, and he could think on these.

He whistled his own tune, a few bars of "John Brown's body lies a-mould'ring in the grave," then stopped. The subject was too morbid.

He began "Yankee Doodle," but the tune was much too sprightly for a tomb.

He next left the stool, dared to approached the near coffin, examined the speaking tube, and like a boy unable to resist, whispered, "Hello," into its flared end. There was no reply. Then, unable to resist the bell cord, which ran down through a hole in the lid, he gave it ever so slight a tug. The bell rang ever so slightly.

Seated again, he thought about the lock of blond hair near his heart, then stopped. It brought a tear to his eye.

He next considered Montfort Morgan, but only for a moment. The subject was too unpleasant.

He wondered for the millionth time who his parents might have been, and why they had abandoned him on an orphanage doorstep. Then he erased the matter from his mind. It had never brought him anything but tears.

He next thought about "rich rewards," then stopped, ashamed. He did what he was doing not for personal gain but because it was the kind, the obedient, the proper, thing to do.

Recollection of the orphanage recalled to him four lines from the only poem he had memorized there, a poem he'd had to recite for the supervisors to show how studious and talented were the children. He was not entirely certain of the meaning of the lines but he liked them. They had become for him a kind of creed. He said them to himself now, over and over:

> "'Out of the night that covers me,
>   Black as the Pit from pole to pole,
>   I thank whatever gods may be
>   For my unconquerable soul.'"

By these means, by using every resource of his youthful spirit, Josh bore an hour, or four, or more, of his vigil. Though spirit be willing, however, flesh is weak, and gradually, minute by minute, hour by hour, the torture, mental and physical, took its toll of him. Cold crept into the very marrow of his bones, and with it, fear. His teeth chattered. His bottom ached. And chills pattered up and down his spine like mice. He commenced to see things. The coffins seemed to move on their catafalques as though there were life within. The walls of the mausoleum seemed to close in on him like those of a prison cell. He thought he heard things. What was that outside? Footsteps? What was that hollow supplication which seemed expelled from the mouth of the speaking tube atop the near coffin? "Help?" He shut his mouth, he shut his eyes, as though in doing so he could stop his ears—but he heard it again, unmistakably.

"Help!"

Help!—the urgent word was echoing—help!—off massive stone and concrete walls—help!—and out of corners distant yet nearby—help!

Josh was off the stool, afghan fallen to the floor, and listening through every pore.

"Help!"

Clang!

The bell of the Bateson's Belfry rang!

Clang!—the echo hurt his ears—clang!—off massive stone and concrete walls—clang!—and out of corners distant yet nearby—clang!

Yes, yes, help and clang and he was out the door and running cramped and stiff-legged, pounding along the sandy track and flying from the cemetery down the street. A block from the mansion he took a short cut, across the bridge over the Deerkill and up a hill to a street lined with imposing homes, among them that of Dr. Hopkins. He reached it, mounted the steps puffing like a good fellow, and turned the doorbell handle. To his surprise, the house was lighted. To his further surprise, Silas Hopkins appeared at once, fully dressed, opened his door, stepped onto the porch, and when he had heard Josh out, seemed not in the least surprised.

"I see." Reflective, the physician tweaked an end of his mustache. "You're absolutely certain?"

"Oh—yes—sir—help!" Josh panted. "And—the—bell —rang!"

Hopkins nodded. "Remarkable. Two o'clock in the morning almost precisely."

"Maybe you—didn't put enough—poison in him, sir."

Hopkins shot him a strange look. "Don't be absurd. I know my dosages." He frowned. "Well, I'll go to the cemetery at once. If there is in fact some sign of life, some function of his organs, I'll attend to my patient. If there is not, we'll chalk it up to your hearing—or your imagination." He put an approving hand on the boy's shoulder. "You have done capitally, Josh. Meanwhile, here's what I want you to do. Listen carefully. Go home, get some sleep. Just be sure you rise early enough to get back to the mausoleum before Eli Stamp shows up to spell you. Do you follow me?"

Josh did not. "But, sir, if Mr. Cadbury isn't dead—I mean, if he's still alive—why would Eli need to—"

"In addition," continued the doctor, "you will relieve Eli again tomorrow night."

"But—"

"Should you hear anything, as you have tonight, or believe you have, or see anything unusual, come to me again."

"But, sir—"

"I'll want a full report."

In utter puzzlement Josh pulled off his stocking cap.

"But, sir, if Mr. Cadbury's alive, why would I have to go back tomorrow night to—"

"And if he is not, at this moment at least? And if he were to cry for help then, or ring the bell?"

"Oh."

Dr. Hopkins raised a finger. " 'Theirs not to reason why, theirs but to do and die'—and that includes you, Josh. Just do as I ask, will you?"

"Yes, sir."

"Peckham, by the way, will have a meeting at ten in the morning, after which everyone will know what you and Eli are up to. And one more thing, Josh. Do not— I repeat—do not mention this episode tonight to anyone. Not a single syllable. Agreed?"

"Yes, sir."

"Stout lad. Good night." The physician smiled. "And pleasant dreams."

Within a minute of his dismissal of the boy, Silas Hopkins, wearing his fur cap and Chesterfield coat, walked with long strides from the rear of his house to his stable. Within another minute he drove out in his phaeton, a two-seater buggy roofed and sided with canvas, which had evidently been hitched to a mare in readiness. Down the hill he went at a fast trot, then through the streets of the somnolent town, turning eventually into the cemetery entrance. Had anyone been abroad at that hour, and in that vicinity, he might have seen the rig stop before the Cadbury mausoleum, the doctor descend, and, carrying his black bag, hurry into the tomb. If this had aroused the curiosity of the observer, if he had continued to watch and wait, he would have been positively astounded by the next development. For after an interval, not one but two persons emerged from the vault—Dr. Hopkins and a small, slight man dressed in a dark suit, a man whom the physician assisted with slow step to the buggy and into it. Then, the reins taken, the whip applied, the two men were trotted rapidly away into the night.

Unfortunately there was no one to observe, gentle reader, but thee and we.

*. . . Miss Cadbury lay on the floor, having fainted dead away . . .*

# 6

# *The Root of All Evil*

rainerd Peckham presided at the meeting in the parlor at ten o'clock that morning. Family and servants were present, except for Eli, whose absence went unnoticed by the nieces. It was another funereal day, cold and gray, but the atmosphere within the room, rather than solemn, was electric with anticipation. The meeting had been convened, it was presumed, to hear read the Last Will and Testament of Lycurgus Cadbury. Above, tiny light bulbs twinkled in two great crystal chandeliers. The wood of wainscoted walls had an eager gleam. Damask draperies at windows almost rustled. Set in a walnut cradle, a globe of the world seemed to the expectant eye to spin upon its axis. Sofas could not sit still. Tables

trembled. The patterns of oriental carpets became more intricate. The vasty oil above the mantel came to life. Lake Erie was stormier now, the warships locked in battle more belligerent, the broadsides louder, and the valiant Commodore Perry, sword upraised upon his quarterdeck, more valiant than ever. Even the grandfather clock, restored to its place but still void of glass in front and face, seemed to tick and wait, tick and wait, mouth open.

Brainerd Peckham had scarcely opened his when Lillian Morgan opened hers. "Is it necessary the servants be here, Mr. Peckham?"

"It is, Mrs. Morgan." He went on to say that his purpose this morning was, on instructions of his late client, to provide certain information.

Excitement changed to resentment.

"Information!" exclaimed Hetta Mae Cadbury. "Aren't we here to hear the will read?"

"Miss Cadbury, we are not."

"I demand to know why not!" cried Mrs. Morgan. "We are his next of kin, and we have every right to—"

"And I am his executor," interjected the attorney. "In that office I act, as I have previously said, only in accordance with his wishes." He gave the gathering a look which would have defeated even the valiant Perry. "If I may proceed."

He proceeded. His announcement was that the will would be read by him day after tomorrow.

"Day after tomorrow!" expostulated Miss Cadbury.

"Day after tomorrow!" expostulated Mrs. Morgan.

"Asinine!"

"Ridiculous!"

"Horsefeathers," grunted Montfort, and gave the globe of the world such a slap that it whirled almost out of its cradle.

Brainerd Peckham explained. Mr. Cadbury's fear of premature burial was responsible for the delay. He had prohibited a reading of his will for three days after his demise, and as a guarantee that death had overtaken him as surely as taxes, had ordered his executor to station his two male servants in the family mausoleum for that period, Eli by day—hence his absence—and Joshua by night.

"Idiocy," snapped Hetta Mae.

"Madness," snapped her sister.

"But if he should return to life?" Peckham countered. "If his fear should by some chance prove well founded?"

"I left my canary at home! She'll starve!"

"I brought a limited wardrobe from the city!"

"Be that as it may," concluded the executor, "I think you will agree that it will benefit your uncle little to equip his coffin with warning devices if there is to be no one at hand to hear his warning."

His logic was unarguable. The ladies sniffed and subsided.

"Young Overland spent last night there, and will carry on tonight and one more. Eli is there now, and will be tomorrow. After that, on the day following, provided there is no signal from the grave, we shall have the will." Peckham pushed back his chair and assumed the perpendicular. "I have nothing more. Thank you and good morning."

It was not a good morning, nor was it to be a good afternoon in the mansion. Rather than being freed from each other—good riddance to bad rubbish— family and servants were to be penned up together two more days; rather than having questions answered, and futures settled, all were to be kept in suspense. They were like players in a play who, having performed the first and second acts, were now made to wait, standing about on the stage in costume, greasepaint caking on their faces, without lines, until the playwright— Lycurgus Cadbury—had written the third. It made for confusion and short tempers, for sensibilities rubbed raw. And none in the house was more confused than Joshua Overland. What was going on? How could he have heard a plea for help from the speaking tube and a clanging bell when only the night before he had witnessed with his own eyes a lethal injection of poison needled into his employer's bloodstream? But it was not his imagination, he had heard the sounds—Josh would have sworn it on a stack of Bibles. What had Dr. Hopkins found, he asked himself, when he went to the tomb last night? Was the dead man alive? If he were, why had the doctor not told Mr. Peckham? The two men were in daily, even hourly, communication he supposed. If the doctor had told him, why had the attorney not announced the miracle this morning? But if the sounds in the mausoleum had been a false alarm, if the cutter king were truly dead, why not read the will at once; why make, and keep, everyone nervous as cats?

The thought of cats sent him forthwith to the stable. He opened the granary door, counting as the animals emerged. He counted but eight. He thought of Montfort, which sent him dashing out of the stable and around its corner toward the river—too late again. He halted. He had passed the culprit lounging against the stable wall, sneaking snuff and spitting splendidly.

"You've drownded more!" Josh cried.

Montfort's grin was Cheshire. "So I have. Five this time. Oh, they knew the jig was up. They set up a jim-dandy yowling in the sack. Only eight to go."

"Well, you cut it out, or—or—"

"Or what?"

"Or I'll tell Mrs. Pumpley, and she'll tell your mother."

"Tell and be damned," responded the heir to great wealth. "Ma hates cats as much as I do. Give me a mean bitch bulldog any day."

The sheer gall took the wind out of Josh's sails. All he could do was maintain a fierce expression.

"What an ignoramus you are." Montfort sneered.

Josh clenched his fists. "You just say that again and see what—"

"I don't chew my cabbage twice. You are, though. I wouldn't stay in that stone pile all night long for love nor money, but you'll do anything you're told to, I guess. If you were told to stick your finger up your nose till it came out your hind end, you would."

"You shut up!"

Montfort drew himself to full height, a head taller than his adversary. "Make me."

Josh thought better of it. "You wait—one of these days," he warned.

"One of these days," Montfort mimicked. He made a wry face. "And that poop Peckham won't even read the will. Stuck out here in the sticks with the hicks for two more—what a bore. And with dear Aunt Hetty. I'd like to feed her canary to your furry friends. Ah, well, there's something good in it."

"What?"

"The old cheapskate's burning in Hell at last." Montfort snapped his fingers. "I hope they pour on the coal!"

Josh was not a tattletale, but in this instance he convinced himself he must make an exception. His pets had been dear indeed to Mr. Cadbury, and at this rate Montfort would soon do away with every one. Josh told Mrs. Pumpley. She was irate. Like an overnight steamer from New York to Albany, she barged into the small parlor, where the nieces were engaged in conversation, and apprised Mrs. Morgan of her son's misdeeds.

"I don't believe it. Montfort has a heart of gold. He'd never—"

"It's true, mum. Nine of 'em. Threw 'em off the bridge in a sack."

"Who said so?"

"Josh, mum."

"You accept the word of a chore boy?"

"I do."

This was not Mrs. Pumpley but Hetta Mae, who was crochetting a doily. "You must put a stop to it, Lillian. Uncle loved those—"

Her sister erupted from her chair like a volcano. "You take the side of a servant? Hetty, how could you!"

And there was precipitated a truly dreadful quarrel between the nieces, who until this point had been on their best behavior—one so vociferous that Mrs. Pumpley retreated into the great parlor and closed the door behind her. Here she would be out of harm's way, yet near enough to eavesdrop through the transom over the door.

"He's a darling boy!"

"He's a devil!"

"He wouldn't harm a fly!"

"When I think of him with my canary!"

"You dislike all children! Because you have none of your own!"

"Better none than one like yours!"

"If my husband, Harry, were here!"

"What husband?"

This sally further infuriated Hetta Mae's younger, more emotional sister. Mrs. Morgan shifted her attack, and as is always the case in conflicts between close relatives, she struck at the enemy's weakest flank.

"All you ever did was crawl over here every month to wheedle more out of him!"

"At least I came! You put in a grand appearance once a year!"

"At least I didn't beg!"

"You didn't have to—you already got three times what I did!"

They circled each other in the small room, having got down now to the crux of the enmity between them: money. It had been the sorest point for years. It had sundered them. Lillian Morgan snatched a lace hanky from her bosom like a stiletto.

"As soon as the will is read, dear sister," she declared, "I shall take the rest of those dratted cats to the pound!"

Hetta Mae aimed her crochet hook. "On the contrary, dear sister. After the will is read, the cats will come into the house and you and Montfort will go out!"

Mrs. Morgan fired her eyelashes. "If that is what you think, you pitiable creature, you have another think coming. Uncle Ly told me on his deathbed—I am to have the bulk of the estate!"

Miss Cadbury did not shrink. "I beg to differ, you overweight shrew. I saw him before you did—and he assured me I will have it!"

"You lie!"

"Liaress!"

But in a twinkling the meaning of their mutual revelation sank into each woman. They stared at each other. They sank into chairs.

Minnie Pumpley slipped away to the kitchen. Her knees and ankles pained her, but she had stayed, dropsy or no, because she would not have missed a word.

Besides the basement, the only other place where Josh and Verbena might meet in private was the cupola, or "sea watch" high atop the mansion, access to which was gained by a narrow flight of steps from the second floor. Here, that afternoon, boy and girl found time for a tryst. That they could not see Troy to the southeast or Albany to the southwest on this gray day did not in the least concern them; they had eyes only for each other.

"Was last night in the bone yard awful?" she asked.

"Not very."

"But weren't you scared?"

"Shucks, no."

She shuddered. "I would be. I'd cry my eyes out— my hair would be snow-white in the morning. Whatever did you do to pass the time?"

"Oh, I whistled and said my multiplication tables out loud and had a good sleep."

How much he longed to tell her about the strychnine and whisper and clanging bell and the run to Dr. Hopkins' house may be imagined. But he was pledged to silence, and Joshua Overland would never violate a vow.

"You could sleep?"

"Sure. I had this, remember." He touched his overalls near his heart. "The lock of your hair."

"Oh." Verbena blushed, and dimpled, and changed

the subject. She was deeply troubled about their future, about what they might do after the will was read and they were dismissed from service. "What will you do then, Josh?"

"Darned if I know."

"Me either. I can't go home—too many mouths to feed already. I suppose I could apply to the cutter works, but I'd hate that."

"Montfort said maybe he'd get his mother to take you back to New York City with them."

"He did!"

Her violet eyes rounded—orbs of such beauty in Josh's view that enlargement could not enhance it. He frowned. He could have bitten off his tongue. "But he talks big. And even if his mother asks you, you have to say no, Verbena."

"Why?"

"You know Montfort. And you know the terrible things that happen to young girls in big cities."

She was dubious. "What things?"

"I won't say," he muttered darkly.

"Pooh."

"Just take my word for it."

"I don't have to. I'm older than you."

They drew apart, and each looked out the sea watch in a different direction, Josh toward the West of dime novels and derring-do, Verbena toward the south, toward the New York of bright lights and men like "Diamond Jim" Brady. She had put her finger on the pulse of their problem. He might love her, but what could a lad of fourteen do about love beyond barking and wagging his tail? She might love him, but at fifteen she knew that as certainly as day follows night, marriage follows love, or should, and in her case must, or she would wear her life away an upholstery seamstress in a cutter works. The years, then, were out of joint for them. One more and she would be brideable; one more and he would be but fifteen, still scarcely dry behind the ears. Seen in this dim light their relationship was hopeless—except that love at any age, in any time, in any circumstance, is never hopeless. Like hope itself, it "springs eternal in the human breast."

As if to give evidence of this, Verbena turned. "Josh?"

He turned, gladly. "What?"

"Josh, what if it comes out the way I think? I mean, if Mr. Cadbury leaves you a lot?"

"Verbena, I told you, I don't even want to think about it. Mrs. Pumpley said we shouldn't get our hopes—"

"Pooh on her. After three nights in a cemetery you'll have earned it. 'Richly rewarded'—remember?"

He planted elbows on the windowsill, thinking. "Well, I might as well tell you. On the way home from the funeral, with Mr. Peckham, he said the same thing —reward me richly."

"Oh, Josh! Both of them—Mr. Cadbury and now Mr. Peckham—and Mr. Peckham knows what's in the will!" Suddenly the little maid-of-all-work commenced to skip in a circle round and round the sea watch, chanting in rhythm with her movements. "Rich—rich

—Josh'll be rich!" She stopped. They appraised each other.

As far as she was concerned, that curly brown hair and cowlick, that cleft chin, those freckled cheeks and nose, made him the handsomest boy she had ever seen.

"If you are," she challenged, "what'll you do, Mister Overland?"

As far as he was concerned, her vivacity and innocence would have melted an iron door.

"I'll ask you to wait, Miss Huttle."

"For what?" she dared.

"For me," he dared.

Montfort smuggled the cat under his suitcoat from the stable into the mansion, up the servants' stairs and past their quarters, down the hall into Miss Hetta Mae Cadbury's bedroom, and through the bedroom into her bath. She was downstairs, he knew. It was the smallest cat among the survivors and would do nicely for his purpose. He first inspected his aunt's personal articles, noting with relish that among the combs and bottles and shell hairpins was a large jar of LaDore's Bust Food (For Developing the Bust), and on its label this slogan: "Hope Springs Eternal!" He next inspected the toilet. It was identical to the one in his bathroom. The flush toilet was a comparatively recent novelty, having been invented less than twenty years before by Thomas Crapper. Those in the Cadbury house were the Pontifex brand, ordered from England. Near the ceiling was a porcelain compartment which stored the water.

A pipe of sizable circumference ran down the wall from the compartment into the rear of the toilet bowl, and under the compartment hung a pull chain with a porcelain handle. The principle was simplicity itself. When one wished to flush, one had but to grasp the chain by its handle and pull, thereby releasing from the compartment gallons of water which torrented down the pipe by gravity into the bowl and out again below through additional plumbing.

Taking the small cat from under his coat, Montfort put down the seat lid, stepped up on it, and by standing on tiptoe was able to raise the lid of the water compartment. Through the opening he shoved the scrawny animal, lowered the compartment lid, stepped down from the seat, raised the seat lid to its normal position, and surveyed his project with gratification. Cats could swim, unless they were gunnysacked, and this one would swim until such time as the occupant of the room wished to flush and pulled the chain. The pipe down the wall from the compartment to the bowl was easily large enough, he estimated, to contain the cat, particularly when it was rushed downward into the toilet bowl by a Niagara Falls of water. All was ready, then. The very next pull of the chain, the very next flush, would set in motion an extraordinary and delightful series of events.

Montfort Morgan smiled, thought about becoming an engineer if he were ever required to work for a living, smiled again when he realized he never would be, left as surreptitiously as he had come, and went to his own room to await results.

Miss Hetta Mae Cadbury was in fact downstairs, in the entry, having rung up Brainerd Peckham on the telephone. She looked round now and then to be sure no one was within earshot, and kept her voice conspiratorially low.

"It was the day I came, the last time I saw him alive," she said. "He told me—and these were his very words—'I'll leave most of it to you, Hetty. You'll be rich.' His very words. Now, I am a woman alone, Mr. Peckham, and utterly dependent on the check you are good enough to send me each month. But something has happened. My sister tells me that Lycurgus told her *she* would have most of the estate. She must be lying. I am so upset, I can't—"

"Miss Cadbury, what are you getting at?"

"Well, I need some assurance, Mr. Peckham. I'm sure you appreciate that. You know what's in the will, don't you?"

"I do indeed."

"Well, then, day after tomorrow's such a long time to wait—in my nervous condition."

"Yes?"

Miss Cadbury looked round her again. "Oh, Mr. Peckham, if you could just say I'm right about the estate and Lillian's wrong. If you could just assure me. Once the will's read, I'll make it worth your while. I'll give you—"

"Madam."

The attorney's tone, harsh, almost angry, brought her up short.

"Madam, you would ask me to breach my trust? To reveal the contents of the will in advance?"

"Oh no, I didn't mean—"

"And suppose your uncle should rise up from the tomb? To learn that I had disclosed—"

"I didn't intend—"

"Then there is nothing more to say, Miss Cadbury. Good afternoon."

She heard the click as his receiver was placed on its hook. She replaced hers, then climbed the stairs to her room, her eyes brimming.

Just inside the great parlor doorway, close enough to the entry to overhear anyone using the telephone, stood Verbena, her ears burning.

"She called Mr. Peckham on the telephone and asked him to tell her what's in the will!"

"She didn't!"

"She did! But I guess he wouldn't. Anyway, I heard every word!"

Mrs. Pumpley sat down at the kitchen table. Across from her, Josh was making an early supper of cold mutton and bread and cheese preparatory to going to the cemetery for his second night's sojourn. The housekeeper needed a moment to mull this latest news, but felt she must admonish Verbena in the meantime. She raised a finger. "I've told you over and over, girl, till

I'm blue in the face—don't eavesdrop. Don't eavesdrop.
Not if you want to stay in service."

The reproof was wasted on Verbena. "Not only that,
but Mr. Peckham told Josh just yesterday, after the funeral, that he'd be richly rewarded for what he's doing.
The very same thing Mr. Cadbury said!"

That she would pass on this confidence so surprised
Josh that he choked on a bit of bread. When he got his
wind, Mrs. Pumpley was speaking to him. "Do you believe it, Josh?"

"I—don't—know."

"That's what happens when you talk with your
mouth full. You choke. Besides, it's not polite."

"Yes—ma'am."

He was finished. He put on and buttoned up his
woolen jacket, wound the scarf about his neck, and
pulled the knitted stocking cap down over his ears. The
stool and afghan he had left in the tomb for Eli's comfort. Verbena and the housekeeper watched him.

"Come here," Mrs. Pumpley said to them. "Here
—one on each side of me."

They took their places, and sitting between them she
put plump arms about their waists. "Now, you listen,
the both of you," she said. "You're dear to me. I speak
sharp to you sometimes, but I have to." Minnie Pumpley looked up into Josh's face, then into Verbena's.
"We'll have work in this house two more days, maybe
three—we can be thankful for that. Then I don't know
what's to become of us. Oh, it don't matter much
about Eli and me—we're old dogs, we've had our day.

But you two are youngsters yet. You've got your lives
ahead of you. So you mind what I say. Don't get
greedy. Money's the root of all evil. You've seen already, right here, how it makes people spiteful and hate-
ful. It can tear folks apart, it can be the ruination of
a whole family. I tell you, waiting for somebody to die
is a pitiful way to live. You do that and you'll get your
comeuppance. So don't be selfish; don't get your hopes
up. And don't you change from nice to nasty. If you
was to ask me, I'd say Mr. Cadbury has fixed for all of
us in his will. He was a hard man, but a righteous one
—he'll give us a fair shake. But that's his business, not
ours." She looked up into Josh's face, then up into Verbena's. "Mark my words—I've lived a long time—the
only real money is the money you earn. The money you
work hard for. The money somebody else has earned by
the sweat of his brow—oh, it'll jingle in your pocket
the same—but it'll taint your character—it'll turn your
soul sour, like cream. So from now on till the will's
read, don't you—"

"Eeeeeeeee!"

The scream, high and prolonged, in pitch and timbre
remarkably like that of Mrs. Pumpley, originated upstairs, from the front of the house. When the three of
them reached the end of their hall, they saw Mrs. Morgan and Montfort rushing into Miss Cadbury's room.
The servants followed, pell-mell, to join mother and
son in Hetta Mae's bathroom. Wet to the skin, a
scrawny cat sat on the toilet seat cleaning itself with its

paws. Her clothing in disarray, Miss Cadbury lay on the floor, having fainted dead away, and was restored to her senses only when a concerned Montfort, who had run for the smelling salts, applied them repeatedly to her nose.

*. . . she turned then, and gliding again, moved as sound-lessly as a ghost . . .*

# 7

# The Second Night: Terror

oshua Overland, fourteen going on fifteen but not, to his mind, going fast enough, had much to ponder this night. Facing the two bronze coffins on their catafalques, he sat in total darkness on the stool, afghan round his shoulders, and tried to occupy his thoughts with such a diversity of subjects that he would be immune to cold and fear. And as the long hours passed, slow as a cortege, his stratagem was quite successful.

Upon relieving Eli Stamp, just as night enfolded the cemetery in sable, he had filled him in on the day's events at the mansion, and was cheered by the old man's interest. He seemed entirely lucid. They talked a bit before the mausoleum, Eli ascertaining that the boy

had done his chores, Josh inquiring if either of the signaling devices, speaking tube or bell, had been used,
then left each other.

He refused to put any credence whatever in what
Montfort Morgan had said about the future of automobiles. Mr. Cadbury had called them "contraptions,"
costly and unreliable when compared to the horse, a
mere fad which would soon fade from the public fancy.
And in any case, the tycoon had been heard to declare,
even if the damned automobubble might provide noisy,
stinking transportation in the summer, it would certainly bog down when the snow fell. The cutter was a
winter necessity. The cutter, as any fool could see, was
here to stay.

Josh also spent some time putting two and two together. Verbena had seen it, he had not. Mr. Cadbury
and now Mr. Peckham—in speaking to him, in asking
him to do "brave things" and "certain favors"—had
both used the phrase "richly rewarded." The only one
who had not was Dr. Hopkins, and he was only the
dead man's physician. Thanks to Verbena, then, the
implication was plain as the nose on his face. There
would indeed be some provision for him in the will. He
would get something—how much he refused to specu-
late. A little would at least give him a start in life. A
little more and he would share with Mrs. Pumpley and
Eli, so that they would not live out their declining years
in poverty. A little more than that and—well, he loved
a little lass with blond hair and a heart-shaped face,
and he might, just might, in a year or so, put one and
one together. Josh put a hand inside his jacket, into an

overall pocket, and touched something infinitely soft, something precious beyond price—then withdrew the hand, ashamed of himself. He simply must not think on these things. Mrs. Pumpley had warned them not to get their hopes up, not to get greedy. It was excellent advice.

Shame made him think of Montfort again. Twice now, confronting the New Yorker, he had clenched his fists and blustered. He must not back down again. A head taller Montfort might be, and trained in the art of self-defense as he bragged, but if he drowned any more of Mr. Cadbury's pets, Josh would have to fight him. It was a matter of honor. The cat in Miss Cadbury's toilet did not count. It had burst out of the bowl clawing and meowing and soaked, no doubt, but alive to lose its nine lives another day. Any more casualties to the river, however, and Josh must fight or show himself a coward.

He looked at the near coffin, at the speaking tube and brass bell on its lid, and was reassured. No one who could endure three nights alone in a tomb could be accused of cowardice. And his employer must be thoroughly deceased. Neither warning device had been used during Eli's watches. And, as Dr. Hopkins had deduced, what he, Josh, had heard last night, the "Help!" and the clanging bell, must have been his imagination, addled and frightened. It had been forty-eight hours now since the injection of poison, and there had not been a single real manifestation of life within the coffin, and that was that. Lycurgus Cadbury was deader than a mackerel.

He slept. Surprisingly, Joshua Overland slept. He had allayed his fear. He had eked out only three hours' sleep the preceding night, and he was tired, for he had done double duty about the house and stable during the day, Eli doing his here.

And he dreamed. And sometime after midnight dreamed a sound.

It was a wail, a wailing. It came from outside the mausoleum.

The wail woke him with such a start that he almost fell off the stool. He listened. It was not a dog in the distance, baying at the moon. It was a human, a fragile, even a more lugubrious, sound.

He trembled off the stool, let the afghan fall, and moved stealthily to the doorway. He peeped from behind the iron door.

There is a difference between fear and terror. Fear sets the pulse to pounding, the knees to knocking, the breath to racing. Terror is fear magnified manyfold. Terror freezes the blood in the veins, makes the heart strike at the ribs like a snake, erects the hairs on the head, and fastens the tongue to the roof of the mouth so that one is rendered mute.

A figure!

A female figure draped in white and staring and gliding down the sand path toward him!

A sculptured maiden come down from atop one of the pillars in the cemetery—a figure of grief and granite—moving, staring, come to life!

Wailing, "Ooooooooo! Ohhhhhhhh!"

Josh was terrified.

If he ran from the tomb, he could be caught. He whirled instead, scrambled across the room and around the far coffin, that of Maude Cadbury, and kneeling to conceal himself, pressed his cheek to the cold marble of the catafalque. He waited.

The wailing, closer and closer, ceased.

His blood was ice.

Then the sound of footfalls, soft upon the marble floor, nearer, nearer.

His heart battered his ribs.

The rustle of fabric.

On his head, under his stocking cap, the hairs were like pins stuck into his skull.

The sound of someone doing something.

Against the roof of his mouth his tongue was sealed as though by mucilage.

Josh had to see. He was dying anyway, of terror, or he was going mad.

He raised himself inch by inch, holding on to the handle of the coffin, until he pushed the merest peel of an eye above the lid.

Hetta Mae Cadbury!

He had but a glimpse of her face, of her hair let down in back, of the white garment she wore, a night-gown perhaps. For she turned then, and gliding again, moved as soundlessly as a ghost out the door and into the enveloping night.

Joshua Overland slumped to the floor and began to sob. He could not help it. He cried because he was fourteen and had been terrified and was too young to make such sacrifice in health and strength and sanity.

His tears trickled down the catafalque. It was as though he were sobbing at the feet of the mother he had never known.

How long he cried is of no moment. When he was drained, and his heart was stilled, he rose again, hauling himself to his feet by the coffin handle. But no sooner had he risen than something caught his attention. Slowly he stepped around Maude Cadbury's coffin, slowly approached that of her husband.

Something white was stuffed into the speaking tube.

He pulled at it.

It was a cheap cotton handkerchief.

She had wadded a hanky and stuffed it into the tube to shut off the air supply to the interior of her uncle's coffin.

He tugged it out, then looked at the Bateson's Belfry. The bell cord, which entered the lid through a hole, had been pulled entirely out of the coffin, and a second hanky had been stuffed into the hole, shutting off that source of air as well. He pulled it out, put it in a jacket pocket with the first, dropped the bell cord down through the hole into the coffin, then stood still, shaking, shivering, making what he could of his discovery.

It was attempted suffocation.

She had sought to suffocate her uncle.

Hetta Mae Cadbury was determined to see that in the event Lycurgus Cadbury had been buried alive, he would have no opportunity to signal the world to that effect. That having been declared dead, he would stay dead. And that his will, in which she expected to be named the principal beneficiary, would therefore be read tomorrow without fail.

Josh was profoundly shocked. This was murder, or attempted murder. If the corpse was not yet a corpse, if the body in the coffin yet contained some spark of life, the woman had made every effort to extinguish it. On the other hand, of course, if the corpse really were a corpse, it was not murder, for how could one murder a dead man? In either case, however, her intent was obvious, and obviously criminal, because Hetta Mae Cadbury had not known, could not have known, whether her uncle were dead or alive.

It all depended, then, on what Dr. Hopkins had found when he came to the mausoleum last night after Josh had run to him with his story about the "Help!" and the clanging bell. Dr. Hopkins, yes! He who had ordered Josh to come at once with a full report should he hear or see anything unusual tonight! See and hear he had! He must run! Now!

Out the door of the tomb and down the sand track and out of the cemetery, he took the same route through the black middle of this night as he had last. Across the bridge over the Deerkill and up the hill he sprinted, reaching the doctor's home in a lather. The house was dark this night. He staggered up the steps, turned the handle till the doorbell fairly pealed, waited while a light went on inside, and waited long enough for his respiration to return to normal. Finally the physician emerged, yawning, in a silken dressing gown, his hair combed, his demeanor as calm and unconcerned as though he had been summoned to a game of croquet on a sunny day in May.

"Well, Josh," he yawned. "You again?"

He leaned against his door as he listened, and when the boy handed him as evidence for his tale two white cotton handkerchiefs, he looked at them, tucked them away in a pocket, and tweaked an end of his mustache.

"Incredible," he said.

"She tried to suffocate him, sir!" Josh bobbed his head for emphasis. "It was murder!"

"No. You may be relieved on that score," said Silas Hopkins. "I went to the tomb last night, directly after you'd come here. I made a thorough examination, and what you heard—the speaking tube, the bell—was as I surmised. Imagination, Josh. Fear does strange things to us. You had a vapor of the mind, nothing more. I assure you, Mr. Cadbury has shuffled off this mortal coil."

"But sir," the boy pointed out, "she didn't know he was dead, not for sure."

"True enough. And her deed was despicable, if not criminal. She is guilty as sin, but there is nothing to be done about it."

"I see."

"So go home to your bed. This has been very trying for you, I know. Just be at the mausoleum again by daylight, when Eli comes to relieve you."

"Relieve me?" Josh blurted. "Relieve me, sir?" This was equally incredible. This was as clear as mud to him. He tore off his stocking cap. "But sir, Dr. Hopkins, if Mr. Cadbury's really dead, as you say, why does Eli have to relieve me? Do you mean—do I have to go back to that darned place again tonight?"

"Indeed you do."

"But why, sir?" So acute was his discomfiture and vexation that Josh could have thrown his cap to the porch floor and jumped up and down on it. "Why?"

Silas Hopkins laid a sympathetic hand on the youngster's shoulder. "Josh," he said, "I claim him dead, but I am not infallible. There are phenomena for which science simply cannot account. I have read in medical journals, on the best authority, of instances in which men and women, in this country and abroad, have been resurrected from the grave as long as a week, even two weeks, after interment. Let us play fair. Mr. Cadbury has. He has asked for only three days and nights of attention. Shall we not accede to such a small request? I think we must."

In spite of himself, Josh's eyes were wet. The prospect of yet another night of cold and dark and terror almost undid him.

"But sir—" he pleaded.

"I know, I know. You bear the brunt. But you are a gumptious lad, you can manage one more stint, I'm sure. And don't forget—your employer promised you a rich reward. I know this for a fact." Hopkins squeezed the boy's shoulder. "A rich reward, Josh. One more tour of duty, and all is done. Then Brainerd is to read the will. The will, Josh."

"Yes, sir," Josh snuffled.

"Good night, then," smiled the physician, putting hands in pockets. "Don't breathe a word of this to a living soul. I cannot impress upon you sufficiently the importance of silence. Sleep well, and look to your future. Conduct yourself tomorrow night as you have this. Should you see or hear anything singular, run to me again with a report. I depend on you, as does Mr. Cadbury—may he rest in peace. 'Say not the struggle naught availeth,' so the poet says, and he is right. It will avail, I promise. Are you up to it, young sir?"

Josh had hung his head in despair. Challenged, he raised it now, and braced himself, and called upon his unconquerable soul.

"I am, sir," he said.

*"Get up, you country bumpkin! Have some more!"*

# 8

# *Enter a Short,*
# *Fair Stranger*

he weather changed. That day, the last December day before the reading of the will, wind from the west blew off the leaden roof of the sky and let in a chilly, cheerless sun. It was an agitated day. Locomotives of wind huffed hither and yon. In the streets of Gilead the shutters banged, hats were snatched from heads and sailed away, shop signs squeaked upon their hinges. Somehow, though, the full fury of the storm seemed to vent itself upon the mansion of the late Lycurgus Cadbury. Windows rattled. Branches of oak trees scraped across brick walls like fingernails on slate. Doors, when opened, slammed shut. And under the eaves, about the gables and dormers and the sea watch, winds yelled like demons and

howled like dogs and laughed like lunatics. They raised hob in the house.

The sisters ceased to speak to each other.

Hetta Mae Cadbury kept to her room and consumed several of Dr. Worden's Female Pills, "A Valuable Specific for Nerve Difficulties."

Lillian Morgan tried in vain to read a romantic novel, and when it would not suffice, descended to the kitchen to tyrannize the housekeeper.

While shuffling past the stable, late for his relief of Josh in the cemetery, Eli Stamp was ambushed by Montfort, who crept up on him from the rear and shouted, "Boo!" So frightened was the old soldier that he collapsed, and had to be fortified with a glass of Madeira wine before he could continue.

Verbena, washing dishes, dropped and broke a Haviland china cup.

Mrs. Pumpley planned to bake a large Lake Erie pike for lunch, and to stuff it with oysters, onions, breadcrumbs, and parsley. In the process of chopping the parsley she chopped her little finger.

Lowest on the ladder, the chore boy was busy as the wind itself, attending to his own routine tasks as well as those of Eli. He was by now in a condition of extreme fatigue. He had managed only four hours' sleep, and the terrifying experience in the tomb the night before had frayed his nerves to the breaking point. His nose itched. His eyes watered. He was weak in the knees. He was actually in greater need of Dr. Worden's Female Pills than was Miss Hetta Mae.

But it was she who took them, and she who sat in an easy chair pretending activity with her crochet hook as Josh built up the fire in her fireplace. She addressed him unexpectedly. He almost dropped the poker.

"Young man."

"Ma'am?"

"You spent last night in the mausoleum?"

"Yes, ma'am."

"Stop what you're doing when you're spoken to. Stand up. Turn around."

He did so.

She peered at him through her spectacles. "I asked you—did you spend last night in the mausoleum?"

"Yes, ma'am, I did."

"And what did you see?"

His nose itched. He scratched it.

"Don't scratch your nose in public. I asked, what did you see?"

Josh sank deeper into carpeting and quandary. He had been directed by Dr. Hopkins not to breathe a word to a living soul; now it was demanded of him by his employer's niece, assuredly one of the heirs to a fortune, that he divulge all, that he jump from the frying pan into the fire.

"Speak up," she said sharply.

On the other hand, even though she was a living soul, answering her question would only be telling her what she already knew; the physician could not find that faithless. And anything to avoid sending her into a snit. Josh drew a deep breath.

"I saw you, ma'am," he said.

"You what!"

"I saw you, ma'am. Coming into the tomb and—"

"How dare you!" she gasped. "There was no one there when I—" She stopped, fell back in her chair, and went paler than ever, if that were possible.

"I was there, ma'am," persisted Josh, afraid she might faint again. "I heard you coming, making those noises and trying to scare me away. But I stayed, and hid behind Mrs. Cadbury's coffin, and—"

"Oh no!" Miss Cadbury groaned. "No, no!"

"I'm sorry, ma'am." And he was sorry for her. She must be in as dire physical straits as he. It was only yesterday afternoon that she had had the encounter with a cat in her toilet. And what greed, what hatred of her sister and nephew, what reserves of will and strength must have been required to take her alone into a cemetery last night, there to undertake the suffocation of a dead man, he could only guess.

"Oh no!" she groaned again.

His eyes watered. He rubbed them. When he could see Miss Hetta Mae clearly, she had covered her face with her hands.

"What did you do when—when I was gone?" she quavered through her fingers.

"I found your handkerchiefs, ma'am. I took them out and put the bell cord back in."

"Dear Lord, I am lost!" she whispered.

Josh shifted weight from one foot to the other. He desired desperately to be gone from the room, but was uncertain whether or not he could leave until he had been dismissed.

"Joshua. Joshua, is it?"

"Yes, ma'am."

She uncovered her face. How wrinkled, how wan, how old she had become since her journey in a hired hack to hear her uncle's dying words; she looked like death itself. He waited.

"Joshua, we must keep this between us. Our little secret." She removed her spectacles and dried her eyes with the doily on which she was at work. Evidently she was short of handkerchiefs. "As you know, I will inherit from my uncle. I shall soon be in a position to help you, and I suspect you'll be in need of help. If you will promise me not to tell anyone about last night, I'll be most grateful—and generous. I'll see that—what I'm trying to say is—in return for—"

"I couldn't take money, ma'am," said Josh.

She sat up angrily. "And why not, I'd like to know."

"I just couldn't, ma'am."

"Then you refuse to promise me—"

"Ma'am, I couldn't take money, and I can't promise." Josh shook his head. Though he would rather have eaten worms, he must tell her the truth. "I've already told."

"You haven't!" she cried. "Who?"

Perspiration beaded the boy's brow. "I can't say, ma'am."

"You tell me! This minute!" Miss Cadbury rasped. "If you don't, I'll have you out of this house ten minutes after the will's read! D'you hear me?"

"I m-m-mustn't, ma'am," stammered Josh.

"I'll have you thrown into the streets! You'll starve!"

"Oh, ma'am, please," implored the wretched lad.

"Go! Leave me, you little lout!" cried the lady, crumpling her doily into a ball. "And have the house-keeper send up a pot of cambric tea!"

But no sooner was he downstairs ordering the tea than they saw Eli Stamp tottering toward the house when he should have been on duty at the tomb. Josh and Verbena rushed out to assist him inside, to help him into a kitchen chair. The old man's hands shook as though with palsy, and it was only after the administration of more Madeira that he was able to speak. He had stepped from the tomb to spit, and had suddenly seen a man, a stranger to him, hiding behind a column at a grave not far away. The man remained, lurking from pillar to pillar, into and out of trees, staring at the Cadbury mausoleum, staring at Eli. The veteran shouted at him to go away, but he continued to trespass and to stare. He was a short man with corn-colored hair and a burly build, wide shoulders and a thick torso. He wore a black felt cap and a black cape with a velvet collar. What his intentions were, Eli had no idea, but he was patently intent on mischief.

Eli was adamant: he would not return to the cemetery alone. It was too early for Josh to take over as sentry. A compromise was reached, and Josh accompanied the aged retainer back to the mausoleum. There, no trace of the mysterious stranger was to be seen, and Eli was at length persuaded to stay on by himself, albeit reluctantly, for the rest of the afternoon. He seized Josh by the shoulders.

"Turrible trouble, though—I be leery in my lumbago, like in the war. You git back soon now. You git back here long afore dark."

He turned to the tomb and saluted. "I'm a-comin', Gin'ral!" he croaked, and marched to the iron door.

Josh plodded toward the mansion, his knees uncertain, his spirit faint with foreboding. He hoped, on reaching home, to steal time for a nap in his cubbyhole.

It was not to be. For as he neared the house, he chanced to glance south, toward the bridge over the Deerkill, and there he saw Montfort Morgan whirling again, swinging a gunnysack round and round. This time he did not run to the rescue. It was too late. And so he watched as the heavy sack flew through the air, and struck the surface of the river with a splash. Then it sank, as did Josh's spirit. He stood where he was, waiting in the wind, the knowledge that the time had come, that he must now fight Montfort without fail, like a millstone round his neck. His eyes watered, almost with tears. Worn though he was, sorely tested in mind and body though he had been day and night, he would neither flinch nor flee. He was honor-bound.

Montfort approached, dusting haughty hands. "Four more down, four to go!"

Josh took his stand. "I told you," he began, then had to shout over the wind to be heard. "I told you! Drown any more and I'd thrash you!"

Montfort snorted. "Ha! And I told you! I'm trained at fisticuffs!" Lips curled in a sneer, he positioned himself opposite and raised his fists professionally. "Just call me 'Fighting Bob' Fitzsimmons!"

Josh squared off and clenched his fists. "You'll be sorry!" he warned.

"Ha!" Montfort commenced to circle his opponent, dancing this way and that in a manner designed to display his fancy footwork. "Come on, chore boy! Come on, you illegitimate good-for-nothing!"

Stung beyond endurance, beyond control, Josh threw caution to the wind and rushed in a red rage at Montfort, swinging a roundhouse right. This the New Yorker sidestepped neatly, and before Josh could regain his balance, he was buffeted by a perfect left hook to the point of his chin. It sent him tumbling.

"Ha!" exulted Montfort. "Get up, you country bumpkin! Have some more!"

Josh rose unsteadily, knowing already that he was overmatched, that his arms were too short and his feet too clumsy, aware that he must grapple with Montfort, get him on the ground somehow so that his sturdier physique might give him an advantage. He squared away again, but by the time he could launch a second assault, Montfort planted both yellow shoes and unleashed a lightning right cross, again to the point of the chin.

Our hero went down like a sheaf of wheat. Lying flat on his back, he saw stars. And as if to add insult to injury, he was suddenly being shaken by the arms like a rat by a terrier, and a woman's face came into view.

"Stop this! Stop it!" she shrieked. "You let my son alone, you bully!"

It was Lillian Morgan.

"But, but, but," Josh mumbled. One of his teeth was loose. His lower lip was bleeding. He raised himself on an elbow.

The matron had let him go, and went now to her son to inquire if he had been hurt. Since he had not suffered so much as a scratch, she sent him to the house to rest from his exertions, then addressed his fallen foe.

"Get up, boy! I wish to talk to you!" She looked about her. "Up with you! Follow me!"

Josh got to his knees, shook his head to clear it, then stood upright with an effort, swaying, trying to bring the woman into focus. Mrs. Morgan had stalked to the stable, and waited for him at the door, a fierce look on her face. He started for her, stumbled, and dropped on a knee. She glared at him, tossed her head, and stamped an impatient foot.

"Do as you're told!" she cried.

He tried again to rise.

"This instant!"

"I abhor a stable," she said some minutes later, sniffing disdain. "But I bring you here so that we may speak in private, just we two. Nothing I say is to go beyond these walls, d'you understand?"

"Yes'm."

Josh enunciated badly. His lower lip was already swollen. They stood near the horses in their stalls, the

four which Mr. Cadbury owned to draw his Prince of
Wales carriage and open loop calash in summer, his
two- and four-seater cutters in winter. Josh was used to
them, but Mrs. Morgan's nostrils were affronted by the
fragrances of grain, hay, straw, and manure.

"Very well," said Mrs. Morgan. "Now then." It was
dank in the stable, and she drew her black wool redin-
gote closely about her. "This is to be your last night in
the mausoleum, is that right?"

"Yes'm." Josh nodded.

"You are to do something," she proceeded. "I want
two things, actually. Around midnight you are to leave
your post for a short time. Take a stroll down the road,
twiddle your thumbs, I don't care what—then return.
But you are to be gone for at least fifteen minutes. Is
that clear?"

"Yes'm." Josh bobbed again.

"The second thing. You are to say nothing of this to
anyone. Wild horses will not drag it from you. Is that
clear?"

"Yes'm." Josh was still be befuddled by the two
blows to his jaw. "I mean, no'm."

"No? No what?"

"I mean, I can't, ma'am."

"Can't what?"

He hated like sin to say. He knew by now the conse-
quences of opposing one of his late employer's nieces—
the recollection of his earlier colloquy with Miss Hetta
Mae was still vivid.

"Well?"

"I mean—well, ma'am, I just can't leave the coffin," he said. "I promised Mr. Cadbury—"

"Mr. Cadbury is dead."

"I guess he is, ma'am. After tonight he will be, I guess," Josh floundered.

"Then there is no reason why—"

"Oh yes, ma'am, there is. Mr. Peckham told me to stay right there by that coffin and listen and—"

"I will hear no more." It was Lillian Morgan's turn to interrupt. She drew herself up, and the pink of rouge on her cheeks was made scarlet by irritation. "You are no doubt ignorant, but surely there is one thing you can get through your looby head. I was Mr. Cadbury's favorite niece. His will is to be read tomorrow, and I will be his principal heir. This means that after tomorrow I shall be in charge of everything here —I shall give the orders. Do you understand?"

Josh nodded dumbly.

"Good. I am beginning today, with you. I have given you two orders. You are to leave the tomb for fifteen—"

"No, ma'am." As Josh spoke, he began to back away from her. "I can't do it."

The matron pursued him, matching each of his backward steps with a forward. "Are you saying—are you saying that, having just assaulted my son bodily, you now refuse to obey my orders?"

He backed into the harness for the Prince of Wales carriage, a complicated maze of leather and iron which hung from the wall of the stable and splayed out onto the earthen floor. "I can't leave the coffin, ma'am. Please don't ask me."

She ceased to pursue. She forced her full face into a smile. "Perhaps I'm not making myself clear, Joshua. Since I will be in charge, I can hire and fire; I can reward and punish. And if you do what I ask, I will be inclined to reward you handsomely. How does that sound?"

Josh scarcely heard her. A tooth wobbled in his mouth with every word he uttered, his jaw ached, his lower lip was twice its normal size, and now he had somehow entangled his feet in the harness.

"I couldn't take money, ma'am," he tried to say. "It wouldn't be right, or honest, to—"

"Balderdash!" Mrs. Morgan's false smile vanished. Her face hardened into those lines which, oils and creams and lotions notwithstanding, herald the advance of age. "You are stupid and ungrateful and vicious and stubborn, and I wash my hands of you. But if you won't listen to reason, perhaps you will to something else." She looked daggers at the boy. "I would advise you not to go to the tomb tonight. I say no more than that. If you have even a glimmering of intelligence, if you care for your well-being, you—will—not—go—to—the—tomb—tonight."

She stabbed him once more with her eyes, to his very marrow, then swept imperiously from the stable.

Josh was left alone at last. He freed his feet from the harness. Wind battered the walls of the building. Near him the horses, a matched pair of blacks and one of bays, stamped and whickered. He put his hands against the wooden bar of a stall, and laid his forehead on it. Last night and this day had been beyond his adolescent power to bear. Miss Hetta Mae had tried to scare him out of a year's growth, then tried today to bribe him and threatened to throw him into the streets and let him starve. On the basis of his lumbago and the sight of a short, fair stranger, Eli had prophesied impending doom. Montfort Morgan, a city whippersnapper, had whipped him soundly in a fair fight. And now Mrs. Morgan, unable to buy his loyalty, had warned him, if he cared for his well-being, not to go to the tomb tonight. It was all too much, and too unfair. It seemed to him that there was no justice anywhere. He felt himself disgraced and persecuted; he deserved the comfort, now that he was alone, of a good cry. He shut his eyes, squeezed out a tear, and was about to let the freshet flow.

"Stop sniveling."

He started up, in surprise and embarrassment. It was Lillian Morgan returned.

"You listen to me," she said, her chin high. "I have ordered you. I have offered to reward you. I have warned you. I might as well have talked to a stick or a stone. I told you, I will also be in a position, shortly, to punish. If I were a man, I'd horsewhip some sense into you. But perhaps you will heed this. I know your situation. You are a ward of the state of New York till you are sixteen, unless someone is responsible for you. My dear, dear uncle has been. My dear, dear uncle is dead, or so we suppose. Look at me."

Josh turned his face to her, one cheek stained by a single tear.

"Unless you remain at home tonight—or unless you

leave that tomb for fifteen minutes at approximately midnight—the very instant after the will has been read tomorrow I will send you back where you came from. To the orphanage."

Just before nightfall the winds ceased to blow, abruptly. After the tumult of the day an eerie, almost a deafening, silence settled over the landscape. A dog's bark startled a street. A pin's drop caused a house to creak. The peal of a church bell hung indefinitely in the ear. If Gabriel's trump had sounded in Gilead, the dead in Troy, ten miles distant, would have risen from their graves to await the Judgment.

Even in the kitchen the usual commotion was abated. Earlier that afternoon Mrs. Pumpley had stuffed and put three chickens in the range to roast for dinner. She took one out now, quietly, and gave Josh both wings for his supper. Quietly Verbena peeled a pile of parsnips. Josh sat quietly at the table, conscious of his swollen lower lip, in a state of such weariness and apprehension he could scarcely gnaw the meat from the bone. No one spoke. Presently Mrs. Pumpley cut a slice of prune cake, put it by the boy, and with a sigh sat herself down across from him.

"Your poor lip," she said. "I watched from the windy here."

"So did I," said Verbena.

Josh could have crawled under the table. "He's taller'n me. His arms are longer."

They murmured sympathy.

"You wait," he said. "You wait till next year, when I'm fifteen. I'll clean his clock."

They murmured agreement.

"I don't like it," said the housekeeper after a time. "Some stranger loiterin' round the mausoleum. What's he up to? What's he after? Who is he?"

No one could say.

"Well, I don't like it, not one little bit I don't. Josh, I wish you wouldn't go back there tonight."

"So do I." Verbena shivered.

Josh picked up the prune cake in his fingers. "I wish I didn't have to, but I do."

"Use your fork," clucked the housekeeper.

"Yes, ma'am."

"Eli's in a stew, too, about tonight. He said so. He said it's how it was in the war, the night before a battle."

"I had my war today," Josh said. "With that doggone Monty, and then with his mother."

Mrs. Pumpley was interested at once. "With his mother?"

"In the stable, after the fight. She told me I better not go to the tomb tonight."

"Why not?"

"Well, what she said was, not if I care about my well-being. Or something like that."

"Your well-being!" The housekeeper blinked her eyes in alarm. "My stars!"

"Why do you have to go, Josh?" Verbena persisted, thinking aloud over the parsnips. "Who'd ever know if you didn't?"

Josh finished the prune cake. "I'd know, Verbena.
Besides, what if Mr. Cadbury isn't dead? What if he
whispered, 'Help!' or rang the bell, and I wasn't there
to hear it?"

"Pooh."

"Eeeeeeeee!"


Minnie Pumpley's scream, in pitch and timbre remarkably like that of Hetta Mae Cadbury's when surprised by the cat in her water closet, careened off
kitchen walls and resonated through the house.

She had half-risen from her chair. She had pointed a
plump arm at the south window. Now she fell backward into the chair, gulping for air with such intensity
that Josh, whose heart had almost stopped, scrambled
round the table to her, and Verbena, who had jumped
six inches off the floor, untied her apron and fanned
the unfortunate woman.

"What's wrong, Mrs. Pumpley?" cried the girl.

"What happened?" cried Josh.

The housekeeper had swallowed her tongue. She
wheezed, she labored, she took in great draughts of air,
but before she was capable of response, Mrs. Morgan,
Montfort, and Miss Cadbury came trooping into the
room.

"What in Heaven's name?" shrilled the spinster.

"Sounded like a damned steam whistle," was Montfort's contribution.

"I demand to know—" began Lillian Morgan.

"A man!" wheezed Minnie Pumpley. "At the
windy!" She pointed. "The stranger!"

"What stranger?" gasped Miss Cadbury, her hand at her throat.

"Aha, the plot thickens!" quipped Montfort.

Mrs. Pumpley had choked, and could not continue till Verbena fetched her a glass of water. When she had drunk it off, she could testify that though it was near dark, she had indubitably seen the head and shoulders of a man peering through the window, a man with corn-colored hair wearing a felt cap and a cape— the very stranger who, by prowling the cemetery near the mausoleum, had that very morning frightened Eli to the house.

"Oh no! We shall be strangled in our beds!" moaned Miss Cadbury, and fled the room.

"Ridiculous!" scoffed her sister.

Montfort snapped his fingers. "I have it! Send the chore boy out. He'll thrash him!"

Verbena could have scratched his eyes out. Josh could have thrust him into a gunnysack and thrown him in the river.

"But I saw him!" insisted Mrs. Pumpley. "Won't nobody believe—"

"That will do!" Lillian Morgan took charge. "Enough is enough, Mrs. Pumpley. You are seeing things. It's probably indigestion, thanks to your own cooking. You will spare us further details and proceed with dinner immediately. I am famished. Come, Montfort, let us have a game of dominoes."

"I've made up my mind," said Minnie Pumpley, after several minutes' deliberation. She sat at the table,

elbows on the oilcloth, chin in hands, flummoxed and
fearful, unable or unwilling to proceed with dinner.
"Josh, you can't go there tonight. It's too dangerous.
You're only a boy, and—"

"He's got to," said Verbena to their surprise. "If he's
to be rich—and he will be—he's got to. And he'll be
perfectly all right."

"All right!"

"Yes." Verbena Huttle dropped her paring knife,
faced her friends, and set her dimples in defiant dots.
"Because I'm going with him," she announced.

Josh was putting on his jacket. He stared at her.
Mrs. Pumpley let down her hands and stared at her.

"Two of us'll be safe," asserted the girl. "This is the
last night; it'll all be over tomorrow. And besides, Josh
and me belong together."

Josh felt his ears flame.

To the housekeeper, the girl's idea was fantastic.
"What about dinner?"

"Eli can serve."

To Josh, the idea was inconceivable, even if secretly
appealing. "Verbena"—he scowled— "not in a million
years would I let you—"

"You have to."

"That tomb's no place for a girl."

"Or a boy, either."

"You haven't had a bite of supper!" This was the
housekeeper.

"You can send something with me."

"You'll be scared," Josh warned.

"No scareder than you."

"You're just a little whiffet!" argued the housekeeper.

"I can scratch. I can scream."

"But what if something happens?" Josh threatened. "Something bad?"

"Then it'll happen to both of us, won't it?"

"I must say, child, you have a mind of your own," Mrs. Pumpley grudged.

"I didn't used to; now I do. Everybody else does." Verbena pushed the pile of parsnips aside and laid her apron on a counter. "There, it's settled. I'll go get my coat." And with a pert, triumphant smile for each of them, she tripped up the stairs.

"Land of Goshen!" breathed the housekeeper, then galvanized herself out of her chair. By the time Verbena had come down again, coat on and a kerchief tied about her head, there was a drumstick and a parsnip and a slice of prune cake for her, wrapped in a napkin. But the cook was having second thoughts.

"I dunno," she muttered, hands on broad hips, surveying the pair before her. "If anything goes wrong, I'll not forgive myself." She glanced at the window in which she had seen the mysterious stranger, shook her head gravely, wiped at her eyes with a hand, then bustled to them suddenly and kissed them on the tops of their heads. "Go along now, before I change my mind. It's late, and Eli's old and cold and hungry. Go along now, dears, and come back to me safe and sound in the morning. And bless you both."

Despite her concern about the short, fair stranger, she went out into the stilly dark, onto the back porch, and watched them into the winter night as long as her eyes allowed. They walked bravely together toward the cemetery, boy and girl, side by side, hand in hand.

"Look out for my darlings, Lord," prayed Minnie Pumpley. "They are all I have."

Then she said, inside herself, to someone else, "And they're about all you have, too—remember that. So you be good to them. You rest in peace tonight, Lycurgus Cadbury."

*Suddenly he was overpowered, seized by arms so much stronger than his own that he could not even struggle.*

# 9

# *The Third Night: Murder*

h, Josh, I'm scared!"

"Verbena, you said you wouldn't be."

"Well, I am!"

"Pretend we're playing house," he teased. "Just the four of us."

"Four?"

"Mr. and Mrs. Cadbury and—"

"Mrs.!"

"Sure, her coffin's right by his."

"No! Oh, Lordy, let's go home!"

"You know I can't."

"Please!"

They conversed in whispers outside the mausoleum, near the open iron door. This night was somehow more dire, more dreadful, than the two preceding. The sky was cloudless. Frigid moonlight flooded the cemetery and, in the midst of death, endowed inanimate objects with life. Branches of trees were bare arms, reaching. Tall granite pillars pointed fingers of shadow at headstones and markers. But the greatest contrast was in the absolute absence of sound. It was more than a silence after wind. It was a funeral hush. It was as though the thousand dead, mourned by the living long ago, this night mourned themselves. Under the soil they stirred in grief, each one, the old, the young, the remembered, the forgot, and shed a dusty tear.

"Verbena, listen," whispered Josh. "If you want to go, you can. I didn't think you should come along in the first place."

That put her back up, and she shook her head. "No. I'm staying. If you've got the spunk, Josh Overland, so do I."

He took her hand again, and led her into the tomb. So brilliant was the moonlight through the doorway that all was distinct, and he could satisfy her curiosity about the coffins on their catafalques, the stained glass windows, the stool against the wall on which he perched, and the afghan on the marble floor. Verbena had eyes mostly for the coffins.

"Which is Mrs. Cadbury's?"

"That one, the one behind."

"What was her name?"

"Maude, I think."

"How—how long has she been dead?"

"Twenty years, Eli said."

"And that's the speaking tube, and the bell, on his. I see. Oh, Josh, what if he said something? What if he rang the bell?" She shuddered. "Lordy, I'd die!"

"Don't worry. He won't," she was assured.

To divert her, he placed her on the stool, draped the afghan about her shoulders, sat down on the floor in front of her so that he had some benefit of the afghan on his own shoulders, and bade her eat her supper.

"What's that smell?"

He sniffed. "Camphor maybe. Eli's sock."

Eli had taken to wearing the sock about his neck while doing duty during the day. One was very likely, he contended, to be "tooken" with the ague in a tomb. Josh and Verbena had met him coming out of the cemetery as they were entering, and the old soldier was in a temper. He berated Josh first for being late, then for bringing a girl with him. It wasn't military. General Ulysses S. Grant would never endorse a female's standing sentry at his grave.

Verbena ate her drumstick and prune cake and gave the parsnip to Josh. "I hate parsnips."

"You'll be hungry."

"No, I won't. I'll be thinking."

"What about?"

"How rich you're going to be tomorrow."

"Remember what Mrs. Pumpley said—the only real money is what you earn. Somebody else's money will turn your soul sour, like cream." Josh nibbled at the vegetable. "I'm not expecting anything."

Verbena stuck to her guns. "Well, I am. You've earned it. Josh, you know nobody would ask anybody to

stay in a scary place like this for three whole nights
and not give him a penny for it. You know that's true."

He, too, hated parsnips. "Well, maybe."

"And I don't think Mr. Cadbury ever liked Hetta
Mae or Mrs. Morgan or Monty. Once I heard him say
they were all 'grabbers.'"

"He did?"

"'Grabbers.' So who does that leave? You!"

"And Mrs. Pumpley and Eli and you."

"But they're old, they don't need much, and I'm just
day help. You're young, and you've done more for him
than anybody." She tugged at the tassel on his stocking
cap. "And didn't he say 'rich rewards'? Didn't Mr.
Peckham, too?"

"Well, yes." He eschewed most vegetables, including
spinach, turnips, and rutabagas. "I guess I might as
well tell you. Dr. Hopkins said it, too."

"He did? Then there!" she exulted. "That makes
three! So 'fess up—you're the one and you know it!
Tomorrow you'll be Mister Moneybags!"

Josh cocked an arm, and like Christy Mathewson, fa-
mous pitcher for the New York Giants, fired the parsnip out the mausoleum doorway. He had to concede
her logic. How wise it would be for a young man to se-
lect a wife as logical, and as common-sensical, as she.
On the other hand, he had learned it was ill-advised to
expect too much of the future; and for an orphan, a
chore boy, a dreg at the bottom of the social barrel, it
was exceedingly dangerous to dream.

"We prob'ly oughtn't to talk about it," he said.

"Pooh. If we don't, I'll freeze to death or fall off this

stool with the frights." Verbena drew the afghan about her closely. "Tell me—when you're rich, Josh, what'll you do? I mean, with the money."

"Gosh, how do I know?"

"Think of something."

"Well, I'd see that Mrs. Pumpley and Eli would be well fixed. For the rest of their lives."

"That's nice. What about the old hags? And dear Monty?"

Josh cogitated. "That's a hard one. I guess what I'd do, I'd give the sisters just what Mr. Cadbury did, and no more."

She nudged him with a knee. "What a soft heart you are. I wouldn't. I'd send them packing, without a red cent. They're the meanest, selfishest—"

"You wouldn't," he reproved.

"Wouldn't I? What do you think they'll do to us if they get the chance?"

Josh was silent. He knew what they would do; an angry Hetta Mae and a cruel Montfort had told him.

Through the knitting of his cap she trifled with his ear. "What about us? I mean, if we're rich," she asked softly.

"Us? Oh, I dunno."

"I do. We won't live in the mansion. We'll have a bigger one, at some ritzy place like Newport."

"Newport? Where's that?"

"I'm not sure. But I've seen pictures. And we'll have a yacht, too, like J. P. Morgan, and sail around the world."

"What do you know about J. P. Morgan?"

"A lot. I can read. And we'll have a golden carriage, with four horses and two coachmen. And, Josh, when we're out for a drive, and we pass Hetty Mae and Mrs. Morgan and Monty walking in the gutter wearing rags, you'll toss them a coin, and I'll wiggle my ears and stick out my tongue."

He smiled, and reflected. "Maybe we won't have a carriage. I might just buy an automobile. Like a Columbia or a Stanley Steamer."

"What do you know about automobiles?"

"A lot. I can read, too."

"Oh." Rapturous, she flung her arms around his head and hugged him. "And you'll use snuff and carry a cane and wear a top hat, and I'll use perfume and carry an ivory fan and wear furs and diamonds and sleep in my own bed and have my own maid! Oh, Josh, it'll be—it'll be—" She sought an adjective appropriate to a lady of style and wealth. "It'll be exquisite!"

She freed his head, and carried away by her vision and its imminent realization, she lay back against the wall of the tomb. Soon he heard her even breathing. She had fallen asleep. It was the best thing for her. But he must stay awake, no matter how bleary and bedeviled he might be. Not only had he watch to keep over Mr. Cadbury's coffin, he now had a slip of a girl to guard as well. Lucky he was to have her company; with her at his back, giving spiritual reinforcement, there was less need to dread the approach of midnight, the hour at which Mrs. Morgan had ordered him to absent himself from the vault. Thinking of that forced him to admit how lucky he had been in other ways. If Dame Fortune had left him in a basket on the doorstep of an orphanage, she had also brought him eventually into the employ of a man of enormous means. She had given him friends—Mrs. Pumpley and Eli and Verbena, who was rapidly becoming much more than a friend. Could she have saved her most lavish blessing for the last? Might the fickle Dame have decided to shower him on the morrow with wealth beyond his most foolish fantasy? Why not? Had he not, in sweat and tears and fidelity and terror and selflessness, truly earned a "rich reward"?

He had, of course he had, as surely as one of Horatio Alger's heroes. And so, upon this pleasant possibility, and despite his resolve, Joshua Overland himself fell asleep. He dreamed of yachts and whatnots and honeypots, of candy and ice cream cones and talking to the high and mighty on big black telephones. He dreamed of marble halls and formal balls and motorcars and ten-cent cigars and cabbages and kings and all shapes and sizes of expensive things. He dreamed of eating it, yet having his cake, and pulling wishbones till they break.

It broke.
He woke.
A wishbone had broken. But it was not a wishbone. He had heard the sound of a twig, stepped on outside the mausoleum, breaking with a loud snap in the silence.
He waited.

He heard another, a second loud snap.

Cramped and trembling, he rose, and carefully, in order not to wake Verbena, he crept to the iron door and peeked around its edge.

In the moonlight a man strode toward the tomb, a man wearing a cap and a cape—unmistakably the short, fair stranger who had alarmed Eli in the morning, and whose face this evening at the kitchen window had so upset Mrs. Pumpley. It must be midnight now, the time when, according to Mrs. Morgan, Josh had better have a care for his well-being.

In three long steps he reached the girl, put a hand over her mouth, and hissed in her ear, "Verbena, wake up! Don't make a sound! Come on!"

Her eyes flew open. As he removed his hand, her mouth opened, then closed as he pulled her from the stool and hurried her to the far side of Maude Cadbury's coffin. Here he pushed her down behind the catafalque, then went down with her to his hands and knees.

"Ssssh!" he whispered, the hairs on the nape of his neck prickling with panic.

Within seconds there was a step on the marble floor. Josh edged forward far enough to see around the corner of the catafalque.

The man stood in moonlight shafting through the doorway. Of less than medium height he might be, but he had broad shoulders and a powerful trunk. He looked about him momentarily. Then, satisfied he was alone, he took from a pocket a pair of scissors and stepped to the near coffin, that of Mr. Cadbury.

A shaking Verbena tried to hang on to Josh, but he thrust her from him, watching.

With the scissors, the stranger cut the cord running down into the coffin from the Bateson's Belfry.

He next removed from another pocket a rag and a bottle. Uncorking the bottle, he shook some of its contents into the rag, saturating it, and stuffed it into the bell-cord hole—the very thing, Josh realized, that Hetta Mae Cadbury had done last night in her attempt at suffocation.

Another rag, another saturation, and just as the man began to block the speaking tube with it, an astounded Josh found himself astoundingly on his feet, advancing round Maude Cadbury's coffin, daring to speak in a voice hoarse with uncertainty.

"Who—who are you? What—are—you—d-d-d-doing here?"

The stranger was taken aback. "Why are you here?" he bellowed. "Damn you!" he boomed, and rushed at the boy.

Josh stood rooted in disbelief.

Suddenly he was overpowered, seized by arms so much stronger than his own that he could not even struggle. The rag was clapped over his face, and a sharp odor burned his nostrils. He fought for breath through his mouth, but something acrid seared his throat. He heard Verbena scream.

"You leave him alone! I love him!"

Josh's head reeled, his lungs exploded, he went weak, he could not escape the pungent rag, he sank, and in a trice a merciful darkness covered him and rendered him unconscious.

Slowly he returned. He lay on the floor of the tomb, its marble cold against his cheek.

He tried to rise, and in so doing discovered Verbena lying near him. He crawled to her, and touched her, and when she did not move, did not speak, he burst into sobs of anguish. She was dead.

He fought himself upright by means of the handle on Mr. Cadbury's coffin. Dizzy, nauseous, grief-stricken, he stumbled through the doorway; his stomach convulsed, and bending over, he retched. His nose, his mouth, his lungs, seemed still to burn, but after a time he breathed again, then found his way back into the mausoleum to view the body of his beloved.

She was not dead! To his joy, she sat up, a hand over her mouth, making strangled noises. He raised her to her feet and, with an arm about her waist, assisted her outside, where she bent and retched as he had done.

She fell against him, and they stood together in the moonlight, restored to each other.

"Oh, Josh!" she quavered. "How terrible! Wasn't that the same man who—"

"Yes, at the window. And the one who scared Eli." Tenderly he touched her heart-shaped face. "What did he do to you?"

"The same as you—it was awful. Grabbed me and put the rag over my face." She shuddered, then got control of herself. "I know what it was, too—chloroform."

"Chloroform? What's that?"

"An-es-thet-ic," she pronounced. "I know because one of my sisters had her tonsils out at home, and that's what the doctor gave her."

"But why would he—"

"It's what they use at the pound, too, to put cats and dogs to sleep. If you get too much, it can kill you."

Josh stared at her. "Kill you?"

"Yes, kill you!"

He turned, and dashed back into the tomb. Sure enough, the bell-cord hole and the speaking tube were stuffed with rags wet with the vile chemical. He tugged them out, and threw them into a corner.

"What's wrong?" Verbena had followed him.

"How long were we chloroformed?" he demanded.

"I don't know. An hour, maybe. Why?"

"An hour? Oh no," he groaned.

"Josh, I don't understand."

"Don't you see? After he did us, he stopped up the coffin with chloroform, maybe for an hour. So if Mr. Cadbury was even a little bit alive, he's dead now."

She tilted her head, mystified. "But he was already dead, wasn't he?"

"Well, sure he was."

"Well, then, what difference—"

"But if he wasn't, it's murder. That man killed him!"

"But you just said he was dead." Verbena looked at

Josh as though he were as loony as Eli. "How can you murder somebody who's dead?"

"Suppose you're not sure," countered Josh. "Isn't that murder, sort of?"

"Murder, sort of?" She retreated a step. "Josh, are you all right? I mean, in your mind?"

That angered him. "Yes, I am. Only doggone it, something else isn't right." To clear his head, he took off his stocking cap. "You sit there on that stool a minute and don't talk to me. Don't say a word. I have to figure this out."

She went dutifully to the stool, drew the afghan about her, and studied him as he began to pace the mausoleum, around the coffins, to the door, around the coffins again, in and out of moonlight, in and out of darkness, cap in hand and forehead furrowed. His first thought was that he should run and report again to Dr. Hopkins; but that would mean leaving Verbena alone here, which she would not accept, or taking her with him, which would vex the doctor. And then it occurred to him that going to Silas Hopkins would be a waste of time. The man would only tut-tut and say, "Really? Chloroform? How interesting," and declare Mr. Cadbury dead beyond peradventure of a doubt and tell his informant to go home to bed. No, this time he would stay where he was, with his ladylove, at least until he could do some deciphering.

Something fishy was going on, Josh was now convinced. He had seen Lycurgus Cadbury killed with poison. Yet the very next night, in this very tomb, Lycurgus Cadbury had whispered, "Help!" and rung his signal bell. The man in the coffin had been alive then—Josh would have bet an arm or a leg on that— and if Dr. Hopkins had come at once to the cemetery, as he said he would, he must have found such to be the case. Then why had he assured Josh that the whisper and bell were merely figments of his imagination? Why, last night, had he been indifferent to Miss Cadbury's attempt to suffocate her uncle? And why, if Josh were to speed to him now, would he be just as unconcerned —and unconcerned he would be, Josh was certain— that a stranger had minutes ago sought to murder the cutter king by means of chloroform?

Joshua Overland stopped pacing.

He stared at the massive bronze casket.

It came to him at last. It came to him in a flash of revelation so sudden, so staggering, so overwhelming, that had he not reached for and held on to the coffin's handle he might have fallen to the floor.

He had been an unwitting participant in a hoax both comic and tragic.

He had been a player in a game in which someone else had made the rules, then kept them secret.

Lycurgus Cadbury had not been poisoned.

He had been buried alive, then unburied.

An old man and a boy had been stationed three days and nights in a family mausoleum not, as they had been told, to be alert for signals of premature burial— except on one occasion—but to ascertain who came hither and for what purpose.

Mr. Cadbury had whispered, "Help!" and rung the bell so that Dr. Hopkins, his accomplice, would come at once to the cemetery—lights had been on at the physician's house, and he had been fully dressed—and take him, alive and well, to the doctor's house, there to remain hidden till the game was over. And there he was now, there he had been since night before last— Lycurgus Cadbury cackling laughter at his fiendish scheme, waiting for the reports of skulduggery at his grave run for him by an innocent servant and relayed to him by his doctor.

"Verbena," said Josh, "come here."

She left the stool to stand beside him.

"Verbena," he said slowly, "there is no one in this coffin."

She thought him daft.

"Oh, Josh," she whispered.

"There is no one in this coffin," he repeated.

"Oh, Josh," she said, "please let me take you home. You need rest, and—"

"This coffin is empty," he said. "Sure, we all heard Dr. Hopkins say he was dead, and sure, we went to his funeral. But he wasn't dead, and he hasn't been in this coffin since night before last."

"What makes you think—"

"I don't think, Verbena. I know. There are things I haven't told you—I couldn't tell you. Things that happened here at night I didn't understand. Now I do."

"Dear Josh." Her voice was tremulous with sympathy. "I'm so sorry. Please let me take you—"

"No," he said. "I'll prove it."

He took a step, and essayed lifting the heavy lid of the coffin, to no avail.

"Josh, don't, please," she begged.

Then he remembered.

"I'll prove it," he said, proud to have penetrated at last the dark heart of the riddle.

Moving sideways, he reached round the lower edge of the coffin. His fingers found the little lever the use of which Timothy Teeple, the undertaker, had demonstrated one afternoon in the parlor.

He tripped it.

The lid flew open with a thud!

The bottom of the coffin rose with a whir and clang and clatter of springs!

Verbena Huttle screamed in shock.

Joshua Overland yelled in horror.

For there—just inches from their bulging eyes—at peace on purple satin—clad in a black suit and white shirt and gray cravat—his hands folded—his mouth open—his porcelain teeth bared in a snarl of rage that even death could not erase—there lay the corpse of Lycurgus Harold Cadbury!

*"Cats!"* . . . *"Cats!"* . . . *"Cats!"* . . . *"Cats!"* . . .
*"Cats!"* . . . *"Cats!"* . . .

# 10

# *The Reading of the Will*

illian Morgan looked at the small gold watch pinned at her shoulder. It was ten minutes until three o'clock, and the will was to be read at three. Her toilette completed, she appraised her image in a long mirror, and was eminently satisfied. She wore the best she had brought from the city, a long dove-gray gown of silk faille with a white lace yoke and gray kid shoes. She turned to see her bustle, which made her behind even more buxom than did her natural endowments, and turned again. On the shoulder opposite the watch she pinned a garnet brooch set in gold, an adornment sure to irk her sister. Mrs. Morgan had earlier determined, once she inherited the bulk of the estate, to double Hetty's monthly stipend, but

had by now of course changed her mind. Hetty deserved nothing, and nothing was exactly what Hetty would have, to the penny. Mrs. Morgan mused a moment, then took up a tiny crystal flask of French eau de cologne, touched the stopper to both earlobes and the insides of her wrists, replaced the stopper, put down the flask, and sniffed a wrist. The cologne had been a gift from Harry, the rascal husband who deserted her. She had treasured it all the twelve long years of his absence. Sniffing again, eyelashes fluttering in ecstasy, she murmured to herself, *"Amour! Amour!"*

In his room Eli Stamp, who was already dressed in his mothball suit and Civil War cap, was having the shivers. His hands shook as though with palsy, and it struck him that this might be an early onslaught of the ague—inevitable, perhaps, after three long December days on guard in General Grant's tomb. As a precaution, therefore, he wet the woolen sock with camphor, wrapped it round his neck under his collar, took a good whiff, and nodded approval of the protective stink.

In his legal office on the main street of Gilead, Brainerd Peckham placed the will and related documents in a briefcase, consulted his turnip watch, found that it was eight minutes before three, and calculated he could walk to the mansion in five minutes. Allowing a minute to don his coat and hat, he was left a margin of two minutes. He prided himself on his punctuality. He intended to ring the doorbell at three o'clock precisely. He leaned back in his desk chair and puffed on a panatela cigar. The attorney was annoyed that he did not know whether to anticipate the reading of the will with relish or distaste. The relatives, insofar as he was concerned, were a worthless lot, while the servants were a mixed bag, some too old and infirm, some too young and green. And while their reactions to their various fates might be interesting, what interested him more was the decision he had made, only this morning, to charge the estate ten per cent of its aggregate value as his executor's fee. This percentage seemed to him fair. His client had been a penurious man. Alive, he had quibbled at every legal expense, however trivial. Dead, he would pay through the nose. Ten per cent would be only just recompense.

Justice, he thought, and smiled, put out his cigar, donned his coat and hat, took up his briefcase, and before going out the door fixed his phiz in its customary somber cast. He made it a policy never to smile in public.

I know she will wear jewelry, said Hetta Mae Cadbury to herself. Very well, so shall I. And so saying, she pinned to the lapel of her black wool suit—she had worn it over from Gloversville and for the funeral—a pink cameo brooch. It was the only piece she owned, and its simplicity would contrast in her favor with Lillian's ostentation. After a sleepless night Miss Cadbury had pronounced sentence upon her sister. As heiress to the bulk of the estate—her uncle's very words—she would cut Lillian off entirely. If the woman had to go to work for the first time in her life, it would be good for her. If the detestable Montfort were driven to pick pockets to buy snuff—she had spied on him from her bedroom window—that would be a profession consonant with his talents. To the servants, especially the snippety chore boy, she had no obligation whatever. They could root hog or go hungry. As for herself, she would live as humbly as ever; but she would give munificently, and anonymously, to the church and to its missionaries in Darkest Africa, those stalwart Christian soldiers who fought for the Redeemer among the heathen. The world might not know of or commend her charity. Heaven, however, would. And a place there would be reserved for her.

Even though it was a bit early, she decided to go down to the parlor now, to be certain of a good seat. Moving toward the door, she found herself warm all over, even hot, on fire in fact. For the sake of her nerves she went into the bathroom, drew a glass of water, and gulped two of Dr. Worden's Female Pills although one usually sufficed. Then she started for the door again, stopped, put a hand to her forehead, returned to her bathroom, drew another glass of water, and gulped a third.

"Eureka!" Montfort Morgan exclaimed. He was standing before the mirror in his bathroom applying bicycle oil, and leaning close, he found what appeared to be an unmistakable fuzz on his upper lip. He danced into the bedroom and threw himself full-length on the bed, bouncing with delight. Soon he would have a handlebar, four inches long and waxed upward at the ends into sword's points. It would excite the envy of every male, and make him fatal to every female. Montfort had never been so happy. The discovery put the frosting on his cake. Fuzz, and in a few minutes, a fortune for his mother! He'd celebrate tonight. Hot diggety-dog, would he celebrate! Having snooped until he located the Cadbury liquor supply, in a basement cupboard which served as a wine cellar, he'd sneak a bottle of the best Madeira up to his room. He'd get drunk as a skunk!

Oh, Lord, prayed Minnie Pumpley, I don't ask a blessed thing of You. Wearing her black Mother Hubbard and white apron, she sat alone at the kitchen table, for so many years her throne and fortress; her hands were folded, her eyes closed. Well, yes, I do, she contradicted herself. I ask that Mr. and Mrs. Cadbury be taken to Your bosom, and that they get along together better there than they did here on earth. And I want You to know I surely hope when Mr. Cadbury wrote that will he was in his right mind and took good care of everybody—myself included, forgive me. He was a hard man, Father—I know that well enough—but he was fair, and I surely hope he has done something nice for poor Eli and that sweet Verbena and my darling Josh. That's all. She paused. No, there's something else, dear Lord. We are about to hear the will, and when it is over, please don't let there be a knockdown, drag-out ruckus. Servants and family, the both of us, let us part from each other in love and goodwill. But if anybody goes away from this house in hate and anger, let them roast in the flames of Hell till they holler. That really is all, Lord, and thank you. Amen.

Riding in his doctor's phaeton toward the mansion, Silas Hopkins whipped his roan mare into a trot. He was several minutes tardy, and determined not to be. He would not miss a minute of the fireworks for a king's ransom. He had telephoned Peckham that morning to be doubly certain of the time. "Three o'clock, is that right?"

"Three, yes."

"By the way, I'll send you my bill for final medical services to the deceased. I assume the estate will pay. I should warn you, it will be steep."

The attorney was blunt. "How much?"

"Oh, five hundred, or thereabouts."

The phone was silent. Then the attorney said, "That is steep for an injection."

"Not to mention several house calls, day and night, and the loss of considerable sleep, and the risk of damage to my professional reputation," answered an irritated Dr. Hopkins. "You wouldn't care to tell me, would you, how much you will slice out of the estate for administering it?"

The phone was silent.

"I thought not. Three, then."

"Three."

Hopkins reined his phaeton into the driveway, and just then saw the tall, spare figure of the attorney ascending the mansion steps. Peckham turned at the sound of the carriage. Hopkins' smile of greeting was not returned. He had never seen the attorney smile.

In her black muslin dress Verbena waited on the side of the bed in her small room. She would go downstairs when Mrs. Pumpley called her. The housekeeper, she guessed, was probably praying, but Verbena did not believe in prayer. She believed in what life had taught her: The Lord helped those who helped themselves. Josh, who was but minutes away from coming into scads and scads of money, could not help. He was only a boy. She was already a woman, and it was she who must lend him a helping hand. She must beware that he was not cajoled or finagled out of his fortune; she must take care that out of the goodness of his heart he did not give it all away to those less fortunate. She must mother and sister him, counsel and guide him, and more than anything, see to it that he grew, in two or three years, into a manhood capable of, and eager for, a happy, loving, lasting marriage. And so she sat on the edge of the bed, waiting, readying her fifteen-year-old self for the grown-up responsibilities which within minutes would be hers. She sharpened her chin, she deepened her dimples, and in her lap she made her small, work-worn hands into fists.

He was darned if he would wait like an animal in his cubbyhole. He had therefore gone down to the back porch to wait, and there, in the cold winter afternoon, tired and tense, his lower lip still sore, in tweed

knickers and knee socks and a wool jacket with a
Buster Brown collar, he was trapped. He could not go
inside because he could see through the door window
that Mrs. Pumpley was praying, and it would not do to
interrupt her devotions. Standing on one foot, then the
other, hands thrust into pockets, teeth chattering, to
keep his mind off how cold he was he thought of everything under the sun, and the moon as well. He thought
of a girl, of rich rewards, of drowned cats, of crashes in
the night, and of pitching for the New York Giants. He
thought of how generous he intended to be to Mrs.
Pumpley and Eli. He thought of how, if he were given
wealth that afternoon in the great parlor, he would
spend whatever was necessary to go to Albany, to the
orphanage, to the police, to trace the identities of his
parents. He thought of prospectors and gamblers and
gunfighters and cowboys and mule skinners and Indians
and scouts and bears and buffalo and all the population
of the wild and fabulous West. Finally, and exclusively,
he thought of bonds and stocks and grandfather clocks,
of building a wine cellar and doing business with John
D. Rockefeller, of dollars and starched collars and diamond studs and tailor-made duds and ebony canes and
fine champagnes and shoes and ships and sealing wax
and palaces full of gold knickknacks.

To himself, Joshua Overland made admission at last.
He wanted these things. He yearned for them passion-
ately, desperately, profoundly.

Behind him, Mrs. Pumpley tapped the window. He
turned, and for a moment they looked at each other.
Then he went to the door and opened it.

"Time, Josh," she said.

"Yes, ma'am," he said.

"Ahem."

Brainerd Peckham cleared his throat and looked solemnly about the room.

"Shall I call us to order?"

There was no need. All were in perfect order—Mrs. Morgan and Montfort and Miss Cadbury facing him from a sofa, the servants ranged in a row near the doorway, Silas Hopkins lounging in an easy chair at the attorney's right hand.

"I believe I will ask that the servants be seated," he said. "This is apt to take some time."

"Seated?" questioned Mrs. Morgan, glancing at her sister's cameo.

"With the family?" questioned Miss Cadbury, glancing at her sister's garnet brooch.

"Yes." The attorney nodded at the four in the rear. "Will you find chairs, please, and pull them close?"

An interlude of milling and pulling and pushing ensued, as housekeeper, retainer, maid, and chore boy arranged seating for themselves at a respectful distance from the relatives.

Lillian Morgan put fingers to her nose. "What is that ghastly odor?" She glared at Eli Stamp, who was nearest her.

"It must be Eli's sock, mum," said Mrs. Pumpley.

"His sock?"

"Yes, mum. He's got it soaked with camphor, and tied around his neck. It's for the ague."

"Well, it's not for me." Mrs. Morgan sniffed. "He simply reeks. He must remove it."

"Do so, if you please, Mr. Stamp," directed the executor.

Mumbling and grumbling, the veteran betook himself from the room into the entry and returned mumbling and grumbling, sans the sock.

"Let us proceed," said Brainerd Peckham. "You may well wonder why Dr. Hopkins has joined us this afternoon, but he has done so at my request. The necessity for his presence will be made known to you presently." Drawing from his briefcase a sheaf of papers, he placed them before him on a small deal table brought from the library for the purpose. "I have before me the Last Will and Testament of Lycurgus Cadbury. I drew it up—"

"Excuse me," said Lillian Morgan suddenly.

"Beg pardon?"

She rose melodramatically from the sofa. "I have a most stunning surprise for everyone—but especially for me!" she burbled. "This may be the most thrilling afternoon of my life, in more ways than one. If you will allow me a moment."

She bustled grandly from the parlor. Those present waited, heard the front door of the house open and close, heard conversation *sotto voce,* then goggled as Mrs. Morgan bustled grandly back into the room on the arm of a short, fair stranger.

"I have the great pleasure," she beamed, "of introducing you to my husband, Mr. Harry Morgan, Esquire. And you, dear Montfort, to your long-lost father."

"Why, that's the man who—" Mrs. Pumpley started, then stopped herself.

The short, fair stranger created considerable stir. The servants looked at one another and squidged uneasily in their chairs. Miss Cadbury assumed an icy disregard. Peckham and Hopkins conferred behind their hands. Montfort, his face sallow with chagrin, extended one of his to his sire and managed an unenthusiastic, "Hullo, Pop."

Harry Morgan cut a dapper figure even without cap and cape. He wore a suit of bright brown flannel, and a blue bow tie with polka dots. His hair was indeed corn-colored, though flecked with gray; his face was smooth-shaven and masculine, his eyes were a matinee blue, and his smile was a statement of white strong teeth. He was shorter than his wife, and shorter than his son, but athletic of build, polished of manner, and even the most malicious among them, Miss Hetta Mae, had to acknowledge him a handsome brute. He had also a roguish air. It was not difficult to conceive of his having run off to the South Seas for a dozen years with his secretary, or of his having perished by foul play in the sewers of Paris.

"I owe an explanation," he said boldly, arm about his spouse's ample waist. "It may be that no account of Mr. Cadbury's passing was sent the papers in New York, but a man of his stature does not die unnoticed. I happened upon a brief obituary in the *Times* day before yesterday, and hastened at once to be with my dear wife in her hour of grief. It is a husband's duty to—"

"Ha!"

Miss Cadbury's scorn was clearly audible. Harry Morgan flushed. Had there been a small object available, Lillian Morgan might have hurled it at her sister. But everyone present understood the maiden lady's ejaculation. As plain as paper on a wall, Harry Morgan had reappeared after twelve years to share with his wife not only her sorrow but her inheritance.

"I apologize for the interruption," he said, his mien abruptly altered. "Sit down, my dear," he invited Lillian, and seated himself between her and Montfort with such male prerogative that Hetta Mae was wedged into a corner of the sofa. He then addressed the executor curtly. "It is understood, I trust, that I shall represent my wife's interest. And now, sir, can we not get down to business?"

Brainerd Peckham's stare was cold. "Indeed, Mr. Morgan. We were so engaged until your intrusion." He gestured at the sheaf of papers. "As I was saying, I have before me the Last Will and Testament of Lycurgus Cadbury. I drew it up at his behest some months ago, and it was then executed—that is, signed by him, witnessed according to statute, and filed with the clerk of the county. That it is a legal document in every respect I can vouch. Do you wish me to read the will verbatim, or shall I dispense with the preliminary matter and go straightway to those clauses which may be of paramount significance? To wit, the various bequests."

He looked round the room rather like an owl reconnoitering a meeting of mice.

"Go to the pertinent parts, of course!" exclaimed Mrs. Morgan.

"Pray do, Mr. Peckham," urged Miss Cadbury.

"Dammit, man, what else?" agreed Harry Morgan.

"Let 'er rip!" exhorted Montfort.

"Very well." With a silver pencil the attorney scribbled something in the corner of the topmost page. "I have made a note that the essential contents of this will were disclosed to those immediately concerned at three o'clock in the afternoon of December 4 of this year, 1899." He put down the pencil. "I begin with the bequests to the servants."

"To the servants?" Miss Cadbury disapproved.

"Yes, since they are minor in scope."

She was mollified. "I see."

"Just a minute," interrupted Harry Morgan. "Before you begin, Mr. Peckham, I think it would be helpful, as the bequests are read, if we could measure them against the whole of the estate. In other words, what is the total value of the holdings, in round numbers? To be blunt, how big is the pie?"

The attorney frowned. "I do not see why that—"

"We have every right," Lillian Morgan reminded.

"We certainly do," seconded Miss Cadbury. For once the sisters were in agreement.

Peckham took up his pencil and tapped an irritated

tattoo on the table. His dislike of Morgan, the interloper, was patent; but he was also acutely aware of his position as executor, for it was with these people, not Lycurgus Cadbury, that he would have to work in future.

"Very well," he acceded. "I cannot be exact. There are too many factors. There are securities, government and corporate, and bank accounts, and real estate, and life insurance. There is this house, and its furnishings. There is, finally, the cutter works itself—the inventory, the building, the accounts receivable—"

"Come, Peckham," Morgan chided.

"You insist?"

"We do."

The attorney sat back in his chair. All others leaned forward in their seats.

"The aggregate value of the estate, after taxes," said Brainerd Peckham slowly, "will be slightly in excess of three millions of dollars."

It was a bombshell. Although the extent of Lycurgus Cadbury's fortune had been the subject of endless speculation, save for the attorney no one had imagined it to be of such magnitude.

"Ye gods!" gloated Montfort.

"Gracious!" whispered Hetta Mae.

Dr. Hopkins whistled between his teeth and made a mental note to double his bill.

"My God," said Harry Morgan.

"How lovely!" trilled his Lillian.

The servants stared straight ahead, unable perhaps to comprehend the amount.

Having enjoyed the moment to its fullest, and enjoyed further the fact that his ten per cent fee for administration would be slightly in excess of three hundred thousand dollars, Brainerd Peckham once more took up the will.

"To the bequests," he said. "I shall read the pertinent clause in each instance. First, 'To my housekeeper and cook, Minnie Pumpley, in recognition of her thirty years of faithful service to me and mine, I give the sum of two hundred dollars.'"

They looked at her. They saw her eyes fill. "Two hundred? Oh." In her lap was a handkerchief, and she began to twist it. "Thirty years? Two hundred dollars? Out of three million?"

Peckham cut her mercifully short. "I read again. 'To Eli Stamp, in recognition of thirty years of faithful service to me and mine, and preceding that, of service to his country, I give the sum of one hundred dollars."

"One hundred!" cried Mrs. Pumpley. "Oh, Eli!"

At the sound of his name, the old soldier understood that something was expected of him. He rose from his chair on decrepit legs, faced the attorney, came to attention, raised a hand to the bill of his infantry cap, and saluted.

"Thankee, Colonel!" he quavered.

Peckham proceeded. "I read. 'As to Miss Verbena Huttle, day help in my household, I stipulate that she be given employment in my cutter works as long as she is suited to it.'"

Josh stole a pitying glance at his sweetheart. Her face was expressionless, but he noted that she had made her hands into fists.

"No money? Nothing?" cried Minnie Pumpley, wringing her handkerchief as though to tear it in two. "The poor child doesn't have—"

"Hush, Mrs. Pumpley, this instant!" remonstrated Mrs. Morgan. "My uncle has been more than generous to his help, always."

"He certainly has," her sister concurred, eyebrows raised at the housekeeper. "What did you expect—strawberries and cream?"

"Ahem!" Brainerd Peckham cleared his throat loudly, pushed back his chair, and elevated himself to his feet, towering to such height that he obscured, in the oil painting above the fireplace, the valiant Commodore Perry.

"At this point I must digress," he said. "An explanation is called for, both of Dr. Hopkins' presence and of several things about which you may have conjectured during the past five days. In this explanation I will require the testimony of the doctor and also of young Joshua Overland, which I will ask of them in due course.

"As I stated previously, Mr. Cadbury dictated his will some months ago. After that time he became increasingly worried about its major provisions—his uncertainty growing to such a pitch that three weeks ago he devised a plan, took me and Dr. Hopkins and Timothy Teeple, the undertaker, into his confidence, and asked our assistance. At first we demurred. We had numerous objections, moral as well as personal, but we deferred eventually to his wishes. As you know, Mr. Cadbury was a man accustomed to having his way."

The attorney rubbed a rueful chin. "I will speak frankly. Mrs. Morgan, Miss Cadbury, you must know that despite his financial support of you since childhood, your uncle had little love for you. And conversely he believed, mistakenly or not, that you had little or none at all for him."

"But I did love him!" swore Mrs. Morgan.

"So did I!" swore Miss Cadbury.

"We resent that, sir!" snapped Harry Morgan.

"These are not my opinions," the attorney was quick to add. "They were those of my client. In any case, as I have said," he continued, "Mr. Cadbury devised a plan—a plan which would settle his mind about the will once and for all, a plan which would determine whether or not his nieces' professed affection for him was real or false. In short, whether they loved him for himself or for his money. This in turn would tell whether what he had done in his will was right or wrong."

The room fell unnaturally silent.

"Let us begin at the beginning," said Peckham. "In the middle of the night of November 29 last, the servants were awakened by a crash and came downstairs to find their employer prostrate on the floor, having apparently suffered some kind of seizure. Is that not so?"

The servants bobbed.

"The truth is, Mr. Cadbury hooked one of his canes around a corner of the grandfather clock here"—he

gestured—"pulled it over, then lay down on the floor
and pretended to be in a comatose condition."

There were murmurs.

"Dr. Hopkins was called for, and after an examination declared his patient had incurred a stroke. Is that
not so, Doctor?"

"That is correct," said Hopkins.

"The truth was, Mr. Cadbury was in as good health
as might be expected of a man his age. Is that not so?"

"That is correct," said Hopkins.

"Mrs. Morgan, Miss Cadbury, you were notified by
telephone of your uncle's critical situation. You came to
Gilead at once, to find him failing fast—or so it
seemed. And while closeted alone with him, each of
you was assured that you would inherit the bulk of his
estate. Is that not so?"

Sister shot a fleeting glance at sister.

"I was," said Mrs. Morgan, fingering nervously her
garnet brooch.

"His very words," said Miss Cadbury, fingering nervously her cameo.

"Very well. That afternoon, all of you, with the exception of Mr. Morgan, were apprised of Mr. Cadbury's fear of premature burial, and you were given an
exhibition by Mr. Teeple of the various signaling devices with which the coffin was equipped." Peckham
searched for words. "I understand that the demonstration was—had considerable effect."

Recalling the horrid clang of bell and the whir and
clatter of springs as the lid flew open and the bottom

of the coffin rose, carrying with it the hapless chore boy, all nodded emphatically.

The executor nodded. "Let me go on to that night, then. In early evening young Overland was asked for by Mr. Cadbury, who told him that after his death the lad would be required to do brave things, and that if he did, he would be richly rewarded. Is that not so, Joshua?"

Josh nodded.

"Speak up, boy."

"Yes, sir, Mr. Peckham."

"All right. Then, at around midnight, according to schedule, Hopkins and I came to the house and admitted ourselves. Hopkins awakened young Overland and brought him to the bedside of the supposedly dying man, there to serve as a witness." He looked hard at the youngster. "Joshua, will you tell us in your own words what then ensued?"

"Ensued, sir?"

"Happened."

"Oh." Josh hesitated. He was embarrassed to his shoe tops. He had never before been asked to speak in public. And there was something else. "But, sir, I promised not to say anything about—"

"You are hereby relieved of your oath of secrecy."

"I am, sir?"

"You are."

"Oh." There was no help for it now. "Well," Josh said, "Dr. Hopkins in-injected Mr. Cadbury with poison and killed him."

This caused a consternation in the parlor too extreme to describe.

"What!" cried Mrs. Morgan.

"Heavens!" cried Miss Cadbury.

"Bully for the doc!" cried Montfort.

"Murderer!" cried Harry Morgan.

Peckham turned to the physician.

"No," said Silas Hopkins. "It was not murder—sorry to disappoint you. Josh was told that his employer neared the end, was in great agony, had begged to be put out of his misery, and that I had so agreed. That I was about to inject him with a strychnine solution. I did of course no such thing. The ethics of my profession prohibit euthanasia, or mercy killing. I did, however, inject him with Veronal, which is not a poison but a barbiturate, a drug which induces deep sleep."

Here Hopkins tweaked an end of his mustache with satisfaction. "I read the European medical journals as well as our own. Veronal was originally developed in Germany by Baron von Mering, a physician and pharmacologist, and by Emil Fischer, a chemist, and was first synthesized by Bayer in 1863. It is a derivative of barbituric acid, and has only recently become available in this country. I gave Mr. Cadbury ten grains— enough, by my reckoning, to render him unconscious for a period of approximately twenty-four hours."

Hopkins tweaked the other end of his mustache. "The dosage was correct, I am glad to say. He slept soundly the remainder of that night and through the funeral the next day—and by the way, for those of you who wondered why the services were held in such haste, you now know why. My patient slept through the procession to the cemetery and through that night until two o'clock the following morning. In other words, ladies and gentlemen, we had not in fact buried a dead man. We had buried a live one—and one in excellent health and full possession of his faculties." The physician inclined his head in what was almost a bow. "Will you take over, Brainerd?"

"Thank you." The attorney let them wait while he ran a finger suspensefully around his celluloid collar. "On instructions of my client I assigned Mr. Stamp to stand sentry in the mausoleum by day and young Overland by night, in case any of the signaling devices should be used. Will you now tell us, Joshua, what transpired that first night?"

"But, sir," Josh faltered. "Dr. Hopkins made me promise not to tell anyone what—"

"You are relieved of that pledge, too," Hopkins interjected.

"I am? Oh." Afflicted by stage fright, Josh began haltingly. "Well, let's see. The first night, sir? Oh yes. I heard, 'Help!' through the speaking tube, and then the bell on the coffin rang."

"Poor boy!" sympathized Mrs. Pumpley.

"So I ran to the doctor's house and told him, as Mr. Peckham said."

"This was the signal, prearranged, that Mr. Cadbury had regained consciousness," Silas Hopkins explained. "I'd been waiting for it. I sent Josh home, got out my carriage, and drove immediately to the vault. My patient was somewhat groggy and weak, but in good spirits, and pleased that all had gone so well. I assisted him from the coffin, took him home with me, and cared for him there. I recall his remark when I put him to bed. 'Now we'll see what Lil and Hetty do,' he said. 'Now we'll see what happens tomorrow night.'"

Had anyone glanced at Hetta Mae Cadbury, he would have marked how pale she had become and how nervously her hand worked at the throat of her blouse.

"Now tell us, Joshua," said the executor, "what *did* take place the next night."

Josh was reluctant. "Do I have to, sir?"

"You do."

The boy swallowed. "Well, sir, I heard a moaning and groaning coming, and it was Miss Cadbury." He could not look at her. "She was in her nightgown. I guess she was trying to scare me off. But I hid behind a coffin, and she came in."

"Then?" Peckham prompted.

"Well, she stuffed a hanky in the speaking tube. And she pulled the bell cord out of the coffin and stuffed another hanky in the hole. I guess she wanted to make sure, if Mr. Cadbury wasn't dead, well, he would be now, by suffo-cating him. So I ran to Dr. Hopkins and—"

"He lies!" Hetta Mae burst from her trap to stand at the end of the sofa. "He lies!"

"Murderess!" Lillian Morgan pointed a finger—indeed, an entire arm—at her sister. "Murderess!"

The accused dissolved in tears. "But—but—Uncle Ly wasn't in the coffin!" she wailed.

"You didn't know that!" Lillian rejoined. "How awful of you, how vicious, to try to—"

"Ladies, ladies!" It was the gavel of Brainerd Peckham's voice. He addressed the assembly. "What we have heard is, unfortunately, what Mr. Cadbury had suspected, even feared, would happen—that one, perhaps both, of his nieces would take pains to ensure that he was dead."

He frowned at Hetta Mae. "I shall not be severe with you, Miss Cadbury. Your uncle has been himself, in a clause from his will, which I now read. 'For my elder niece, Hetta Mae, who has for fifty years begged and sniveled and pretended a fondness for me she did not feel, I set aside in trust sufficient funds to provide her for life with the one hundred dollars monthly she presently receives—and nothing more. Further, upon her death these funds in trust shall revert to my estate.'"

Those in attendance stared as one at the old maid. And as the implications of the clause came clear to her, as she understood that for the remainder of her existence she would live as she had, on the razor's edge between gentility and poverty, Hetta Mae Cadbury sank slowly to the floor. But she did not swoon. Forehead against an arm of the sofa, she wept almost silently, mumbling, "No, no, no."

"It serves you right, Hetty," commented Lillian. "I'm delighted our dear uncle saw through you long ago, as I did."

"Come now, Mrs. Morgan," chided Peckham. "Let us proceed. Joshua, I call upon you again, this time to relate the events of your third night in the mausoleum —last night, that is."

Once again the boy became the focal point of attention. But now, strangely enough, what had hitherto been an ordeal for him became tolerable, even enjoyable. For in the interim it had occurred to him that of the four servants, bequests to only Mrs. Pumpley, Eli, and Verbena had been read; and that of the two nieces, the hopes of Miss Cadbury had now been dashed. That left Mrs. Morgan and her son. Could it be that the reading of the will was a process of elimination? Would they all, one by one, fall by the wayside, leaving only himself and the bulk of the estate?

This time he stood. "Yes, sir, Mr. Peckham. Well, yesterday afternoon Mrs. Morgan got me in the stable and said I should leave the tomb for a while last night."

The matron blanched, and sprang to her feet. "That is ridiculous!"

"Did she say why?" Peckham pressed.

"Yes, sir. She said if I cared about my well-being."

"Untrue! Untrue!" cried Mrs. Morgan, her bosom heaving.

"This ragamuffin is an unmitigated liar," growled Harry Morgan. "Calm yourself, Lillian."

"I see," said the attorney. "Proceed, Joshua."

"Well, sir, last night Verbena went with me to the cemetery, and around midnight it must have been, we heard somebody coming, so we hid behind Mrs. Cadbury's coffin and waited. Well, it was Mr. Morgan here."

Morgan bounded from the sofa, his handsome face red as a beet. "You little scoundrel! I'll kill you!"

"Don't touch him!" Brainerd Peckham boomed. "Lay a hand on him, sir, and I shall summon the town constable!" He turned to Josh. "Go on, boy."

"Well, sir, Mr. Morgan cut the bell cord into the coffin with scissors. Then he soaked two rags with chloroform and stuffed one in the bell-cord hole and one in the speaking tube. Then I jumped up and—"

"Harry, how could you!" demanded his wife.

"How could I?" Morgan roared. "Because you told me to, that's why!"

"Murderess!" cried Hetta Mae, roused from her weeping.

"I am not!" defended Mrs. Morgan. "Uncle wasn't in the coffin!"

"You didn't know that!" countered her sister.

"Ah, but he was!" This was Silas Hopkins, who leaped up suddenly to stand beside the attorney. "What I have to report now, ladies and gentlemen, is incredible but true. The morning after I brought Mr. Cadbury to my home from the vault, I found him in the bathroom, on the floor. He was dead, having succumbed of a massive heart attack. The enactment of his plan had been, I venture, too much for his years and frailty."

He shook his head. "I ask you, ladies and gentlemen —what was I to do, how was I to respond to such a calamitous turn of events? There could be but one answer. I did what any man of sense and prudence would do. I loaded his body in my carriage, covered him with a blanket, drove him to the cemetery, and placed him in his coffin—which was where he now belonged, permanently."

"I don't believe it!" cried a confounded Lillian Morgan.

"I don't believe it!" cried a confounded Hetta Mae Cadbury.

"It must be true." This was Josh, ready, willing, and able to provide the denouement. "Because after Mr. Morgan chloroformed the coffin, he chloroformed me and Verbena, and when we came to—well, I got to thinking maybe that coffin's empty, maybe nobody's in it at all—so I tripped the lever and the darn thing flew open and there he was—deader than a doornail!"

"Ohhhhhhhh!"

This was Lillian Morgan. A tragedienne to her toes, she threw up her arms and tumbled like a ton of bricks onto the sofa, half-crushing the amazed Montfort. She had fainted dead away.

Now the great parlor was in total turmoil. Luckily, Miss Cadbury had brought smelling salts with her, should the occasion require them, and by dint of repeated application by Dr. Hopkins, Mrs. Morgan was revived and assisted to her seat on the sofa by her solicitous husband. But no sooner were her eyes open than a relentless Brainerd Peckham again took up the will of Lycurgus Cadbury.

"Madam," he said sternly, "far be it from me to judge either your character or your deeds. What we have heard is exactly what Mr. Cadbury expected to hear after his return to the world of the living—that like your sister, you had been at pains to ensure his demise. Some time ago, therefore, he passed sentence upon you in this testament. I read it to you now. 'For my younger niece, Lillian, who has for forty-five years cried and complained and wasted my substance and called me a miser behind my back, I set aside in trust sufficient funds to provide her for life with the three hundred dollars monthly she presently receives—and nothing more. Further, upon her death these funds in trust shall revert to my estate.'"

Mrs. Morgan's head fell against the sofa back. "Oh, Uncle!" she mourned. "How could you do this to me?"

"Curses!" snarled her husband, rising to face her. "Lil, you were stupid when I married you, and you haven't improved a damned whit. I'm leaving!"

"You beast!" wailed his wife. "You said you came back because you love me!"

"Love you, you fat-assed frump?" Morgan's voice dripped contempt. "Impossible! Farewell, Lil, forever!" And so saying, Harry Morgan adjusted his polka-dot tie and stalked in high dudgeon from the room.

"Oh, he's gone again!" bawled Mrs. Morgan. "Whatever, ever shall I do?"

"It's all right, Ma," her son consoled. "I always knew Pop was an utter cad."

"Montfort!" Realization had come to Hetta Mae Cadbury like a lightning bolt. "Montfort! He's going to get it all!"

Montfort brightened. "Why not?" he smirked, examining his fingernails. "Who deserves it more? Who can spend it faster?"

"I'm sorry," said Brainerd Peckham. "I'm sorry, young man. But I regret to inform you that there is no mention of you in the will whatever."

Montfort's face went black. He sat up, and sent a splendid spit at the corner of an oriental rug. "Damn him," he said. "I'll drown every cat in Christendom!"

"But I don't understand," said a confused Miss Cadbury, supporting herself with a hand on the globe of the world. "If it isn't going to Montfort, then who? Who?"

Everyone gaped at everyone else. And then, almost simultaneously, the same notion transfixed seven of the nine in the room. Seven heads swiveled, fourteen eyes were drawn to the same person as though by a magnet.

The orphan chore boy sat quietly, modestly, a slight smile at the corners of his mouth as though he had just swallowed a goldfish. He had not seen Harry Morgan stalk from the parlor. He had not heard Miss Cadbury's question. He sat oblivious to everyone and everything, daydreaming of marble halls and formal balls and motorcars and ten-cent cigars and ebony canes and fine champagnes and a name to which he might at last aspire, the name of Joshua Overland, Esquire.

"It's Josh!" squealed a delighted Mrs. Pumpley. "Dear, brave Josh, who's done it all!"

She spoke for relatives and servants. For now they knew it must be true.

"Well, well, my lad." Miss Cadbury forced an effusive smile. "I'm sure you'll be generous to those of us who—"

"And don't forget your friend Monty," Mrs. Morgan

gushed. "Surely you'll feel kindly toward him, and toward me for that matter. We—"

"Ahem." The executor cleared his throat, but this time gently. "I propose now to read that clause in the will pertaining to Joshua Overland. I read as follows: 'Joshua Overland is my legal charge until he is sixteen. In my judgment he displays the same sterling qualities of character and the same promise I did myself at his age. It is essential, however, that he learn the value of hard work, and sacrifice, and discipline, and most important, that he not be spoiled by riches early in life, which might incline him to sloth and dissipation. I give him, therefore, together with my gratitude and best wishes, a twenty-dollar gold piece.'"

Brainerd Peckham sat down.

Miss Cadbury sat down.

The whole world, both poles and the equator, came crashing down about Josh's ears.

"Twenty dollars!" cried Mrs. Pumpley.

"Ha-ha-ha-ha!" Montfort Morgan threw himself on the floor and rolled about, his sides splitting with laughter. "Twenty measly smackers!"

And then a new voice was heard. Verbena stood white-faced, repressing her anger. "I don't understand, Mr. Peckham. If Josh isn't to have it, who is?"

"I am coming to that, young lady," was the reply.

"Then come to it!" cried Miss Cadbury, shooting to her feet with remarkable agility.

"Yes, come to it!" cried Mrs. Morgan, catapulting herself from the sofa with flaming cheeks. "Stop play-

ing cat-and-mouse with us, sir! This instant! We can
bear it no longer! We are flesh and blood!"

"Very well, madam." Deliberately the attorney took
up the sheaf of documents. "I shall not read in their
entirety the many clauses which dispose of the bulk of
the estate," he said. "With your permission, I shall con-
dense them into a few words of my own. Ahem." He
cleared his throat. "After those bequests already made
today, Lycurgus Cadbury has set aside every dime and
dollar of his fortune to establish a permanent and phil-
anthropic foundation for homeless animals. Announcement to that effect will be supplied the newspapers
tomorrow. It is to be known hereafter as the 'Cadbury
Foundation for Unfortunate Felines.'"

A stunned and total silence, not unlike that in the
mausoleum, descended on the great parlor. Persons and
chairs and sofas sat or stood uncomprehending. Walls
darkened with disbelief. Chandeliers dulled at the dis-
closure. The grandfather clock seemed to tick and think,
tick and think.

"F-f-felines?" stammered Josh, who had never heard
or read the word.

"Cats!" screeched Hetta Mae Cadbury.

"Cats!" shrieked Lillian Morgan.

"Cats!" howled Montfort Morgan.

"Cats!" mewled Minnie Pumpley.

"Cats!" hissed Verbena Huttle.

"Cats!" exclaimed Dr. Hopkins.

"Precisely." Brainerd Peckham surveyed the room
and smiled. "Stray cats."

"Why don't it snow?" croaked Eli Stamp.

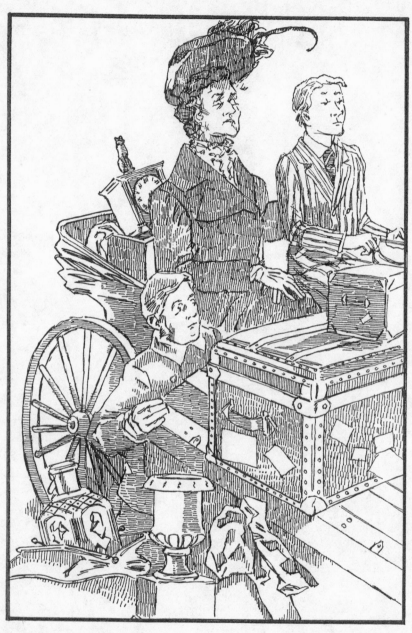

*"Let us be off . . ."*

# 11

## Charity Begins at Home

t did snow, the following day, a few tentative flakes, but no one took much note. The family would depart that day. The servants were allowed to remain in the mansion another night, but only one.

There was a great deal to do. The house, as Mr. Peckham had explained, was to be headquarters for the Cadbury Foundation for Unfortunate Felines, but since there would be a delay of several months while the will was probated, among other tasks the oriental carpets must be rolled up and every stick of furniture covered with protective sheeting.

In the midst of this, Miss Hetta Mae Cadbury declared her intention to leave forthwith, and not only that, to take with her the set of Haviland china. This provoked a fierce fracas between the sisters, but Hetta Mae was not to be denied, and in the end it was Josh and Verbena who had to pack as best they could the entire set, numbering more than one hundred fragile pieces. Her hired trap was then driven to the front door and loaded. On the discovery that there was yet a little room in the rig, she ordered that some of the staples be brought from the larder, and she succeeded in having put aboard a sack of flour, two of sugar, and finally one of oatmeal, which she theorized would sustain her canary for some time.

"Good-by, you old bag!" shouted Montfort as the heavily laden trap lumbered out of the drive.

Miss Cadbury heard him, and turning her head, gave as good as she got: "So long, you snuff-eating snot!"

Eli Stamp was of no help to anyone. He sat about lamenting his lumbago and refighting, for the edification of those who would listen, every Civil War campaign in which he had seen action. He was to be exiled tomorrow to the county poor farm near Gloversville, and he was so informed, again and again, but evinced not the least understanding. The old soldier had previously slipped into partial senility, but now, three days in a tomb had bereft him of the last vestiges of reason.

It was a mercy, said Mrs. Pumpley, sniffling. It was a mercy he did not know, could not know, where he would prattle away his final days on earth. She gathered up the belongings in his room. She found, besides his clothing and toilet articles, eighty dollars in Confederate money, a medal for valor in combat, and wrapped in a woolen sock, a dried tapeworm.

Mrs. Pumpley herself spent a good portion of the day at the kitchen table, unable to do half what was needed, her shoulders slumped, alternating homemade homilies on making the best of life with orations on Lycurgus Cadbury's cheapness. The heart, she said, had gone out of her. She would take the train from Albany to Detroit the next day, there to reside with an elder sister who was "ailing and poor as a church mouse." And with her she would take her life savings, not quite a thousand dollars, which would certainly never see her to her grave. Perhaps she could find housework, perhaps not; she was too old; no one would have her.

"I told you so, I told you so," she would sniffle and wag a finger at Josh and Verbena as they busied by. "Don't wait for folks to die. Earn your own. You remember now, and learn your lesson: Wood you cut yourself warms twice."

Early in the afternoon, Montfort swaggered into the kitchen. "I've done it," said he with a sneer.

"Done what?" inquired Verbena.

Montfort looked hard at Josh. "Drowned every damned one of the damned cats."

"You haven't!" gasped Mrs. Pumpley.

"I have," said the New Yorker. He pointed heavenward as he took his leave. "That'll show the old son-of-a-b——."

Shocked beyond words, the housekeeper collapsed over the table and flooded a pudding.

They had not, however, seen the last of the Morgans.

Mrs. Morgan presently appeared to give a series of orders. Her late uncle's largest coach, an open loop calash, was to be harnessed to a pair of his best horses and brought to the front door. She and Montfort would drive it to Albany themselves, sell it and the animals, and there entrain for New York City. In the meantime she wished every piece of Waterford crystal and every piece of sterling silver in the house to be prepared for cartage.

"The crystal I can sell as is," she said, holding a cold compress to her forehead to relieve the headache she had endured all day. "The old silver I shall have melted down and sold for whatever it will fetch. Now do as I say, this instant. You are still under employ, and if you care to be paid for today, you'd best be quick about it."

It took two hours. Josh hitched up the calash, drove it to the door, and found in the stable another store of gunnysacks. Verbena and Mrs. Pumpley—the latter hoping aloud the wrath of God would one day lay the looters low—did most of the packing. The crystal pieces they wrapped individually in tea towels, then bundled in blankets. Since it was to be melted down, the sterling silver they dumped like cats into gunnysacks and tied the tops. There was flatware service for twenty-four; there were serving platters, soup tureens and ladles, vegetable bowls, creams and sugars, serving spoons, nut bowls, candelabrum, gravy boats, epergnes, salvers, and even a dinner bell. When Verbena rang this last item, Mrs. Pumpley first shuddered at the sound, then herself melted down with emotion. This was the sterling upon which hundreds of hours of spit and polish had been lavished over the years, solid sterling that Lycurgus Cadbury had purchased especially for the presidential dinner in 1882. Chester A. Arthur had been served from this silver. And as the massive, lustrous pieces went bumping and clanking into the sacks, they were well hallowed with the housekeeper's tears.

The calash was loaded. Josh and Verbena toted downstairs and piled on the six valises and four hatboxes belonging to the Morgans. Montfort appeared, recollected the wine cellar, and ordered the last two cases of Madeira brought up and added to the treasure. This was done as well, just as Lillian Morgan descended, weak and wan, to be boosted onto the high front seat by her adoring son, who mounted beside her and took the reins. Maid and chore boy waited respectfully on the steps. Mrs. Morgan straightened the pheasant feather on her hat and pulled her brown beaver coat closer against the cold.

Montfort smirked at Josh. "Twenty measly smackers," he derided. "Like to flip heads-or-tails for 'em?"

Lillian Morgan addressed the servants. "See that you don't strip the house. I have warned Mr. Peckham to keep a sharp eye on you."

Montfort winked at Verbena. "Ta-ta, tootsie. If you ever come to New York, and want a wild old time, give me a tinkle on the telephone."

"Let us be off," directed his mother.

Montfort clucked to the matched pair of bays, and

when they were hard put to pull the coach, which was crammed as full as a freight car, he gave them the whip until they were under such duress that, as the calash rumbled out of the drive into the street, both poor beasts broke violent wind.

As darkness fell that evening, Brainerd Peckham came to the mansion, asked for Josh, and said he would wait in the entry. Spent and grimy, the youngster joined him there at once.

"Ah, Joshua, I have something for you," announced the attorney, reaching into a vest pocket and presenting Josh with a coin. "There you are, my boy—your employer's bequest to you."

Josh turned it in his hand. The twenty-dollar gold piece was somewhere in size between a half and a silver dollar. On one side the American eagle spread its wings; on the other the figure of Miss Liberty held high her torch.

"I trust you are grateful. Mr. Cadbury was a just and generous man."

"Yes, sir. Thank you, sir."

"I hope you will hold on to it," counseled the attorney. "'A fool and his money are soon parted.'"

"Yes, sir."

"Whatever you do, do not fritter it away on trifles—treats and such."

"No, sir."

Peckham buttoned his coat. "Now, Josh, you must be ready at nine o'clock in the morning. Sharp."

"Sir?"

"I will drive you to the orphanage myself. I have

been in communication with them, and you are in luck
—they have a place for you."

Josh's eyes filled. "Oh, sir, do I have to?"

Peckham frowned. "Have to? Of course you do. It is
the law."

The attorney's voice tolled in the entry, sonorous and
deep as a bell, and at the sound Josh shivered and
closed his hand tightly on the coin.

"Oh, sir, Mr. Peckham, mayn't I stay here in Gilead?" he implored. "I'm almost fifteen; I can look out
for myself. Mayn't I stay here and rent a room and
work at the cutter works till I'm sixteen? I want to
something awful, sir! Mayn't I?"

"You may not." Brainerd Peckham clapped his
Homburg hat on firmly. "Nine o'clock in the morning.
And be on time, boy—I shall be."

The chore boy tried to control a swollen, quivering
lower lip. "Yes, sir," he said.

*There in cold and dark and wind and sorrow they clung to each other . . .*

# 12

# "O Grave, Where Is Thy Victory?"

innie Pumpley lay in her bed, listening. A wind of night and winter brushed tree branches on brick walls. In the room next to hers, oddly, there were no old man's sounds. She twisted and turned, and heard the bedsprings squeak. This was the bed in which she had slept for thirty years, and never would again. This was the house over which she had presided domestically for thirty years, and from which she would be cast out tomorrow, never to return. How long had it been since the oak tree toppled? An hour? How long had it been since the four of them started up at the crash of a clock, and went downstairs in fear and trembling to find Mr. Cadbury fallen to the floor? A decade? She

could no longer tell time. It told her. It told her in inexorable terms that she was part of the past, and this she could bear now with balance. She was cried dry. The future lay near her down the hall, sleeping soundly in the persons of her sweet Verbena and her darling Josh. She had high hopes for them. If they had learned well the lessons of this frantic, lunatic week, they would find a way to wait for each other, to join themselves one day in holy matrimony, and then to live happily ever after. As for Eli, dear dotty Eli, in the room next to hers, she had a different hope. To be consigned to a poor farm, to eke out his days in shame and squalor rather than in dignity and pride, was an end the old soldier did not deserve. And so a compassionate Minnie Pumpley wished for him that tomorrow would never come.

She got her wish. For ancient Eli Stamp there would be no shame, no poor farm, no tomorrow. On creaking into bed this night, he had drifted into a perfect slumber and, better yet, into a lovely dream. He was young again, and parading with the Second New York Zouaves down Fifth Avenue on his way to Washington and war. No minié ball had found his shoulder yet; no blood and cannon roar had lamed his spirit. He was young again, striding with his comrades in their hundreds; the sun was shining, fifes and drums were playing, the colors streamed, a mighty throng throated them down the avenue. And marching thus, on the way to war, he was not aware that his heart had stopped, or that his limbs grew cold. On and on marched Private Stamp, young and strong and immortal, and did not know it was a dream from which he would never wake.

Fully dressed even to coat and kerchief, Verbena waited for the tap on her door. If the waiting had not made sleep impossible, hatred would have. She had never hated anyone so much as she did the dead Lycurgus Cadbury—not for herself but for Josh. To jump a boy through hoops of horror, to tease him and freeze him and seal his lips and frighten him out of his wits and promise him rich rewards, then pay him with a crumb and pop him back into a public institution—grrrr. And to think she must work her fingers to the bone in the old miser's cutter works because she had no other prospects—grrrr. The thought of it made her hands into fists again. She hated herself, too, for she was in large part to blame for Josh's downfall. All of last night and all of this day she had been ridden with guilt. It was Verbena Huttle who had got his hopes up, Verbena Huttle who had dared a chore boy to dream of becoming something better—Miss Verbena Huttle and no one else. What would he do now? What could he do? His horizons were no wider, no brighter, than hers —probably less in fact, for he was younger and lacked her perspicacity. She knew only that he intended something, that he had asked her to dress tonight and await his tap on her door.

In his cubbyhole at the head of the stairs, by the light of a small bull's-eye lantern, Josh had been assembling his worldly goods. He had a comb and a toothbrush, a clean union suit and six dollars in greenbacks, a willow whistle and a jackknife, three dime novels

about the adventures of a fearless scout who led the
United States Cavalry against a murderous band of
redskins and a handful of marbles, and a miniature
Bible given him by Mrs. Pumpley on his fourteenth
birthday. These he tied up in a red bandanna, and
then, pulling on his jacket and stocking cap, opening
the lantern case and blowing out the flame, he crawled
with the bandanna over the straw tick and into the
hall.

He stood, listening. Mrs. Pumpley must be asleep. He
moved down the hall like a mouse. There were no
noises from Eli's room, so the veteran for once was
sleeping peacefully.

He reached Verbena's door. If she had done as he
asked, she would be ready.

He tapped.

They crept downstairs and tiptoed through the
kitchen. Opening the door, they crossed the porch, and
once outside, he took her hand and walked with her
across the yard. The night was dark and cold and
windy, no stars were to be seen, nor a moon, and an
occasional snowflake touched like fingertips their faces.
As soon as they were a safe distance from the mansion,
Verbena stopped.

"Josh, where are we going? What are you doing?
You've got to tell me!"

"All right," he muttered. "I'm not going back to that
doggone orphanage tomorrow."

"I was sure you wouldn't. Well, what, then?"

"I'm going out West."

"West? You're not!"

"Yes, I am. Tonight."

"How?"

"Well, I've got it all figured out. I've read about men called 'hobos.' They catch rides on freight trains, in the cars, and ride for nothing. It's called 'hopping a freight.' So I'm on my way to the railroad tracks—it's only a mile or so—then I'll hop a freight going west and be far away by morning."

"But that's dangerous!"

"What do I care?"

"Oh, Josh," she said.

"And I just wanted to tell you and have you walk partway with me so we could say good-by."

She bowed her head. "Oh, Josh."

"So come on." He took her hand. "We can talk as we walk."

She let herself be led. "What're you going to do to-morrow?" he asked.

"Go home, I guess." She sighed. "It's crowded, but they have to take me in. Then I'll go over to the cutter works and get my job—six days a week, ten hours a day for practically nothing. I hate like poison to go, but I don't know what else to do. I haven't any money." She shook her head. "Never mind about me. Whatever will you do out West?"

"Well, I'm not sure," he admitted. "But I've read up on it. I might strike gold or start a stagecoach business or trap for furs. But whatever I do, I'll earn my own. I won't wait around for somebody to give me something. I tell you, Verbena, the sky's the limit out West, and if you're a good man, you can get rich in two jerks of a lamb's tail!"

"Rich," she said bitterly. "This is every bit my fault. If I hadn't told you you'd be rich, you'd—"

"I'd what? Go back to that orphanage tomorrow? The heck I would!" He squeezed her hand. "No, ma'am, nothing's your fault. I've thought about the West a long time. And I owe you a lot, Verbena. You've given me some sand. Oh, I was pretty down in the dumps after the will was read and all today, but I've grown up a lot in the last week, and—"

"Where are we?" She stopped them again, and peered about her. "Oh, Lordy, isn't that the cemetery?"

He grinned at her. "Sure is. I'm cutting through it—it'll save me five minutes."

"But how can you even set foot in it again?" She shivered. "Won't you just die?"

"Shucks, no."

"Well, I'm not going another step!"

"You don't have to."

And with these words, both realized it was time to part. They fell silent.

"What's that in your hand?" she asked.

"My stuff."

"Oh."

From faraway a train called, its sad summons borne to them upon the wind. It matched their mood. It had been child's play to be boy and girl together; but to be man and woman, and to be in love, and to say farewell on top of that, were tasks for which maid and chore boy were unprepared. He looked long at her, at the dimpled, angelic face framed by her kerchief. She looked long at him, at his cleft chin and freckled nose and brave brown eyes.

"Will I—ever see you again?" she murmured.

"You better," he said firmly. "Here's what I thought. I'll go out West and get cracking, and in a year or two —it won't take long—I'll have money coming out my ears. Then I'll send you some through your folks, and you can come out and join me and—and—you will wait, won't you, Verbena? Right here?"

"Oh yes!" She came close to him. "Forever and a day!"

"Then here's something for you," he said, taking an object from a pocket and thrusting it into one of hers. She followed it with a hand.

"What is it?"

"My twenty-dollar gold piece."

"No!" She was aghast. "Josh, you can't, you'll need it!"

"No, I won't," he assured her. "I've saved up six dollars, right here in my bandanna."

"Six dollars! That won't even—"

"Remember, I'm hopping a freight, and when it stops, I'll go by shanks' mare." He tried to smile. "You'll need it more. If you're at the cutter works, it'll be a while before you're paid. Maybe with twenty dollars you can move out of your folks' house and be on your own. Please take it."

She made a small whimpery sound. "But I don't have a thing to give you."

"You already have."

"What?"

He put a hand over his heart. "You've forgotten, but I haven't. A lock of your hair."

"Oh!"

Then, as a blossom bursts from the bud by miracle into full bloom, Joshua Overland and Verbena Huttle were unencumbered of their childhood, and burst into a new and miraculous maturity. She flung her arms about him. He folded her in his. There in cold and dark and wind and sorrow they clung to each other, breast to breast, murmuring endearments through their tears. "Josh darling!" "Verbena dear!" They did not kiss, for a kiss is ofttimes superfluous. And then, as impulsively as she had embraced him, she freed herself in sacrifice, turned from him, and ran away into the night.

He watched her vanish, swiped a sleeve across his eyes, and swinging bundle stoutly at his side, marched like a young soldier on parade toward the entrance of the cemetery.

So tightly did Verbena grip the gold piece in her pocket that it warmed her hand and arm and even her long way home. Twenty dollars! She had never before had half that much at one time. Dear, generous Josh! How she loved him! But then, halfway to the mansion, she had the idea, and she almost skipped. Why should she go to her parents tomorrow and beg them to give her bed and board again when there was not enough to go around? At fifteen a girl should be independent.

And why, for that matter, should she slave at a machine in a factory, growing old before her time? It was all very well to earn your own, as Mrs. Pumpley prated, but if something extra came your way, you should take every advantage of it. She had the means now to do whatever she wished, and a world bigger and brighter than Gilead beckoned. If Josh could have a vision, so could she. Besides, even though he would succeed out West—she was sure of that—it might be years before he sent for her, years she was determined not to waste.

By the time she reached the back porch, Verbena Huttle knew exactly what she would do tomorrow. She'd say good-by to Mrs. Pumpley and Eli and pretend to be going to her parents. Instead, she'd go to the train station and buy a one-way ticket to New York City. It couldn't cost more than a dollar or so. Once there, she'd find a room and search for the Morgans, Mrs. and Montfort. They'd help her obtain domestic work, possibly even in their own household. After all, Montfort had taken a personal interest in her already. And once established in New York, that most exciting of cities, who knew what might happen, who could predict what might await her? Twenty dollars! Dear, dear Josh!

The cemetery could hold no more terrors for him, he was certain, and so he walked the sand path through it without the least trepidation, swinging his bundle and whistling to himself. Dear, dearest Verbena! How he loved her! That she would wait for him, and that he

would soon strike it rich out West and send for her and
hold her in his arms again and stand with her before a
preacher, he had every faith.

He stepped out smartly. In only a few minutes he
would reach the tracks of the New York Central, and
while a boxcar might not be a covered wagon, it would
do as well. A few snowflakes floated by, and he caught
one on his tongue. Eli would be glad in the morning to
see the snow. To the thousand dead about him, to the
bare trees sighing in December wind, to the pillars
topped with urns and crosses and robed, ghostly figures,
he paid little heed. When he reached a point below the
mausoleum, however, he paused. *"Until the Day
Break, and the Shadows Flee Away"* read the inscription over the door. The words had a particular per-
tinence for him tonight. It was he, Josh, who was
fleeing away, and it was he for whom a brand-new day
was breaking.

Reflective, he was somehow drawn from the path up
the knoll toward the vault. Here it was that he had
passed three awful nights, here had done courageous
duty. He approached the iron door. It had not yet been
closed and locked. He stood before it, studying his sen-
sations as carefully as he had the gold piece when it
was given him by the attorney. Did he hate Lycurgus
Cadbury? He should, but somehow he did not. On the
contrary, he pitied him. Why?

There flashed into his mind's eye his last sight of the
cutter king, lying in repose on purple satin—except that
he had not been in repose. The face of the corpse had
been contorted by a snarl of rage. And a perception

came to him. He understood the snarl of rage, but only now. He pitied the old man because, in the end, his plan, cunning and horrible though it was, had gone awry. Mr. Cadbury had failed. He had been right about his relatives, and consequently right about his will, but he had never found it out. He had died—actually died in Dr. Hopkins' house—before the villainy of his next of kin could be reported to him. Lycurgus Cadbury, then, had gone to his Maker without the final, crucial knowledge whether he was right or wrong about the disposition of the legacy it had taken him a lifetime to amass. He had condemned himself to an eternity of doubt. He could never, ever, Rest in Peace.

The chore boy stood for a moment more, musing on the old man's misadventure. He squinted through the doorway, and could discern the outlines of the great bronze coffins side by side. If he listened, might he hear again a whisper through a tube? The clanging of a bell? The whir and clatter of springs lifting a lid with horrid force?

He smiled.

He had just turned to go when suddenly there issued from the interior of the mausoleum, magnified by stone and concrete walls, hurled from corners distant yet nearby, this sound:

"MEEEEOOWWWWWWWW!"

In his veins his blood was curdled.

On his head his stocking cap was raised.

In his chest his heart leaped like an affrighted animal.

Joshua Overland took to his heels. Through dark and

cold and wind and snow he ran with all his might in the direction of the railroad, though there was no reason to run. He knew the sound.

Montfort Morgan, too, had failed in his slaughter. Lycurgus Cadbury might be dead at last, but one of his grieving pets survived—indeed, had triumphed—would live out its nine lives in the lap of luxury!

Josh ran, and somewhere in the cemetery dropped his bundle, but neither comb nor greenbacks nor marbles nor Bible would have stayed his flight.

He fled from his boyish self, from fear, from greed, from lies, from hate, from tears.

Headlong he hastened toward a new land, a frontier of smiles and songs and friends and courage and wealth and love and, above all, of truth.

He ran, carrying with him only the clothes on his back and his unconquerable soul.

## THE END